"Well then, let me tell you something about grenades," Moss said. "That little gadget you have in your pocket has the explosive force not only to take Roger Hilton to hell, but some innocent old lady passing by, or some schoolgirl and a priest who happen to be in the same public place. Grow up, Adam! It can maim a great many people, and still leave your precious Roger Hilton intact. Surely you've seen enough war movies to know that the only way to protect the crowd from a grenade is to smother it with your own body, and there's no way in hell you're going to get Roger Hilton to fall on a grenade."

"Doctor," said Adam, "if there is a theoretical way, and if there is sufficient motivation—there is always a way to engineer it."

He paused for a moment, smiled, and said, "And if there isn't, I've always got the automatic rifle."

LAST RIGHTS

a novel by

H. H. Dooley

FAWCETT CREST • NEW YORK

For David

LAST RIGHTS

Published by Fawcett Crest Books, a unit of CBS Publications, the Consumer Publishing Division of CBS Inc., by arrangement with Doubleday and Company, Inc.

Copyright © 1980 by Doubleday & Company, Inc.

ALL RIGHTS RESERVED

ISBN: 0-449-24392-3

Printed in the United States of America

First Fawcett Crest Printing: April 1981

10 9 8 7 6 5 4 3 2 1

Prelude

September—twenty-two months before the convention

> Former President and Mrs. Roger Hilton celebrated their thirty-fifth wedding anniversary at their home in Hilton Head. Attendance was limited to the immediate family and a few neighbors, according to Jim Doyle, Mr. Hilton's aide (Associated Press release)

"I had managed to assemble the machine gun from its disparate parts with a dexterity that astounded me. After all, I have had no experience with weapons of any sort. I certainly had never hunted as a child. My father found the whole idea distasteful, and was contemptuous of the kind of people who could see it as even tolerable, let alone enjoy it as a sport. I suppose my general understanding of mechanical things made it natural and easy for me. But how had I managed to assemble those heavy parts? And, my God, they were heavy! I could feel the weight of each piece, as I lifted it up, in the swollen joints of my elbows and shoulders. And with each movement to assemble the gun, the pain would shoot through my spine into my lower limbs. How in the world had I managed, crutches and all, to drag this monstrous load through the streets, and into the train station?

"It was a train station, wasn't it? By then I wasn't even sure of that. The pain was so great. All I had left was a sense of a mission over which I had no power of alteration or modification. I was reduced to an instrument, a device, a servant of my own obsession. The plan, once conceived, seemed to move me rather than I moving it. I was its creature now. My creation had become my master. It was almost automatic, I was doing that which had to be done. At that point I couldn't have even articulated what it was that had to be done. There was only the sense that it had to be done and the automatic responses necessary to do it. I continued the assembly and the mount. It was amazing that in a busy train station—yes, now I am sure, it was the train station—people could watch a crippled man fumbling with his crutches, assembling this 'thing,' this contrivance, and do nothing, and say nothing, and suspect nothing. Was it not obvious that it was an instrument of death? Why did no one come up to prevent me? Perhaps it was not obvious. Perhaps it was simply the anonymity of New York. *Was* this New York? I wondered. Did I even know where I was? Of course it was. I didn't remember having traveled out of the city. But then, how had I even arrived here? I remembered none of the antecedent events. I was simply 'there'—wherever there was—and it could have been anywhere.

"Through all the confusion, all the pain, my fingers, those ailing fingers, seemed to be moving their independent way to complete the task. What was the task? Did I know or would it be done without any perceptual knowledge? Slowly the gun took shape. The one thing I was sure of was that—wherever I was—I was in the place I had to be, at the time that had been planned. This was my 'Appointment in Samarra.' I smiled that I should think in such cliché terms at such a time.

"And then, at the prescribed moment, The Evil appeared. By that time my *mind*, that part of me which had always been central to my sense of self, had become a passive instrument of my body, that aching, sick body which even in health had always been seen as an instrument, not an essential part of me. But my mind was servant to a purpose that commanded reason, commanding me; my body was now in charge, driving me, controlling me, humiliating me. I was enslaved, trapped in that sick body which was now directing my life.

"I had no idea what that evil was. Was it a person? A group of people? A blight? A plague? A thing? A fantasy? A delusion? No matter whether I knew. The mission was the message. The mission would be done.

"And then my target came in sight and all doubts disappeared. 'It,' whatever it was, must be destroyed and it *would* be done, and I would do it. With that recognition that the mission would be a success, the pain left. The unabating, incessant pain was gone. That pain which was so woven into the fabric of my life that I could not remember that life was not always pain, the pain actually left, or at least seemed to. Does it make a difference if pain only seems to leave? If it seems to, then I suppose it has.

"And then—would you believe this, Doctor?—there, in the public space, about to do—what, I did not even know—I felt a surge of sexual passion. For the first time in how long—five months, eight months?—I actually felt aroused. The sexual feeling washed through my body like a wave lapping up the shore. This body, I thought, belongs to a man, a real living animal-creature; and at this moment of destruction, I felt alive again. I felt a man again. You understand what I am saying, Doctor. I actually had an erection. I was physically once again a man.

"But the hands, and the eyes, and the fingers, unabated and automatically pursued the carefully orchestrated program which had been so meticulously prepared. The Evil was now in my sights; and now within range; and I reached for the trigger. I had come to the final moment for which all before had been merely prelude. But where was the trigger? Where is the trigger in a machine gun? Isn't it where it is in a rifle? Isn't it there to be squeezed? My hand started groping across the stock. How does one fire these machines? Surely, with all my planning, with all my arrangements, I must know *that!* There was no trigger! Or was it that my fingers were numb? Or was it that I had become paralyzed? Or was it that I had died? Or was it that I was crazy? Oh, God, where is the trigger? It cannot be. All this planning. All this work. All this pain for nothing. Is it to end for nothing? Is it to end with nothing? And the noise. What about the noise? How can I think with that awful noise. The screaming.

Stop the screaming, I begged, so I can think. I've got to find the trigger. It cannot end with nothing. It cannot end in failure. I've got to complete the mission. Stop the screaming so I can think. 'For God's sake, won't somebody stop that screaming!' I shouted.

"And then it stopped. It was I who had been screaming. Sarah had me in her arms. Her hand was over my mouth. It was she who had stopped the screaming. Now she was wiping the sweat off my face. What is she doing here? I wondered. In the train station.

"I was not yet awake. I did not want to be awake. Gradually awareness forced its way into my consciousness and brought with it the wracking, ever present pain, and I knew there was no train station, no gun, and no mission; that I had been dreaming. When that dream ended, when it left, it took with it the residue of my desires. What remained was the impotence, the frustration, the hopelessness, the sense of the mission uncompleted, the job that would never be done. I knew that the pain would be with me till the end, that finally it would consume me, and that, indeed, my mind was gradually becoming enslaved by, and would eventually be destroyed by my decaying body.

"And, Doctor, whatever you say now, that dream told me that this cannot go on. I can't—I won't—endure it. I don't know what the dream means literally; emotionally I know exactly what it means. I don't want to bother interpreting it. It is funny, however, how our childhood fantasies cling. The form might change, but never the substance. And even then we cling to the shred of early forms. If only I could have been St. George—how I wanted to be St. George! But as I grew older, I learned that there were no dragons; and later I would learn that there are no saints. But then I discovered metaphor—and once again I assumed somehow I would find some way to be St. George, that somewhere there would be a dragon to be slain.

"Why is it, Doctor, that we children are raised on heroic myths when life these days is so unheroic? Doesn't it seem cruel? Doesn't it encourage gratuitous and cruel punishment?"

It was particularly at times like this that Dr. Peter

Moss—Professor of Clinical Psychiatry at Cornell Medical School and a practicing psychoanalyst—was thankful for the tradition of the couch. The young man stretched out before him could not see the anguish on the doctor's face, the sweat forming on his upper lip, or detect that mixture of horror and despair which he now felt, and also knew must be showing.

My God, what can I do for him? he thought. What do I have left to offer? How can I make whatever time he has left endurable? How can *I* endure it?

The last thought shocked him. It showed how far he had strayed from the psychoanalytic process. He was concerned about his *own* pain, his own capacity to handle the situation. He had reached the limits of his professionalism. Of course he always felt for patients. That nonsense of the detached psychoanalyst was taught in school, only to be forgotten with the approach of the first patient. But the control of one's own emotions, the unreadiness to let one's own needs intrude on the purposes of the patient, that *had* to be there. For years it had operated well for him, and he had become smug and self-satisfied. Whenever he heard of the behavior of colleagues that implied a breach in that self-discipline, he responded with unsympathetic contempt. Now he felt his confidence slipping, and he was frightened. He was frightened by the intensity of his involvement with this young man. He had had dying patients before; they were never easy. But this was a dying boy, a child, really. Twenty-three was too early to meet death.

Adam Haas was the son of a German-Jewish father and a Catholic mother. His parents had fled the Nazis in 1937, leaving behind the father's fortune, and the rest of his family who refused to abandon the "Motherland." The family had been entirely destroyed, and Adam's mother had always visualized it as being symbolically, at least, her family who had destroyed them. It was then that she renounced the Catholicism which had been her support through childhood and which she had refused to abandon at the time of her marriage.

On arriving in this country Adam's father proceeded in a remarkably short time to amass an even larger fortune. He was an investment banker of extraordinary prescience, great courage and a considerable amount of luck.

They had three children, all girls, when, to their surprise and delight, with the youngest daughter thirteen years of age, the father in his late fifties and the mother in her late forties, Adam was born. He had an extraordinary beauty as a child, which none of their daughters possessed, and was the darling of their older age.

The household being essentially one of women, Adam had at least four mothers besides his own. The three sisters doted on him and the governess adored him.

His mathematical aptitude became apparent by his fourth birthday, although the extent of his genius was not yet clear. By his ninth birthday he was doing calculus, and by his twelfth he had taught himself projective geometry and modern algebra. His parents were determined he should lead as normal a life as possible and they detained him at home in a preparatory school well beyond the age he could have, and perhaps should have, been in college. By sixteen it became ludicrous to pretend his education was continuing at Collegiate, a preparatory school on Manhattan's west side, and he left for Harvard. By nineteen he had his bachelor's degree and by twenty-one his doctorate in mathematics. He always had an interest in mechanical things and was immensely adept with his hands. He was attracted to the concrete applications of mathematics through the world of physics and accepted an appointment at Columbia as an Associate Professor in the Department of Physics.

He had outgrown, to his great satisfaction, the almost feminine beauty of his childhood, but was still enormously attractive, although without any self-awareness. A slight, ash-blond young man, he looked boyish now, not feminine. And one suspected he would have carried those boyish looks through his entire adult life. At twenty-one he had that amiable ability to charm, and an ease with people of all ages, that is characteristic of a child raised among adults. He was enormously popular with both faculty and student body. He seemed in every way the golden boy that might have been predicted at ten or twelve. Externally he seemed blessed by nature and fulfilled through achievement. But all was not well. Terrified and guilt-ridden over sexuality for reasons he was unaware of (indeed, even the emotions were not evident to him), Adam, at twenty-one, had had no sexual contact with a woman—even of the most trivial sort. He sought treatment, presuming that he must be somehow "a latent homosexual." What he was in actuality was a still beautiful infant unable to assume the adult role. It was not manhood which terrified him but adulthood. While, by all outward standards, he had achieved the kinds of success which mark the man, his inner perception was of a world in which he was still a child relating to all women as maternal figures.

New York in the 1970s was an agony for him. Always an aggressive city, the emerging sexual revolution added a new element. He did not need to seek sex; women maneuvered, clawed and pawed their way to him and the advances only intensified both his hunger and his dread. He was always sure he was "projecting" or misreading. The more seductive a woman became, the more sure he was that she was just being friendly and that he was sexualizing all of these encounters because of his own wickedness.

A childhood memory of sisterly affection which aroused and sexually excited him had left its residue of guilt. The fact that the sisters, themselves, might have been just as sexually excited never occurred to him. When Dr. Peter Moss first suggested that these advances on his sisters' parts were a mixture of maternalism and adolescent sexual titillation on *their* part, he was appalled. It never had occurred to him that his sexual responses to his sisters could have been provoked, and beyond that enjoyed by them.

Peter Moss was an incurable optimist, almost arrogantly proud of his therapeutic capacities. Therapeutic failure was interpreted as a personal humiliation; he would not tolerate it.

Adam Haas was an ideal analytic case. He was intelligent, young, pliable and sensitive, with the kind of problem "made for analysis." In addition, Moss was particularly good with troubled young men. He had no sons of his own, and that, he felt, was part of his success in treating this group. They were his sons, and he poured the kind of energy and devotion into them that he might have to his own. At the same time he was involved in none of the counter-transference that might have occurred if he had confused or fused the images of these young men in his own unconscious with his own sons.

Within four months of starting treatment, Adam had an incurable, hopeless crush on an "older woman," Sarah Pedersen. She was thirty-three years old, a successful money manager, and one of the only women on Wall Street to operate her own hedge fund. His idealization of her compounded his anxiety, and his dreams had alternated between those of castration and impotence, and those of heroic power. It was either "the triggerless gun" (a recurrent dream in one form or another since adolescence) or St. George slaying the dragon with his enormous lance and saving the beautiful princess.

Within five months of this hopeless infatuation, Adam was "seeing" Sarah. Six months after meeting her, he had his first sexual experience with her; in ten months he was her lover; and within a year he moved in. Four months after that, he developed the first symptoms of the Ewing's sarcoma that was now killing him. It was part of the tragic irony that so shortly after achieving his manhood he should be dying of a tumor so closely associated with childhood. By the time the pain and swelling in his knee was called to a doctor's attention—a squash injury, Adam had assumed—multiple lesions were detectable throughout his body. Cure, despite all treatments, was out of the question, as the doctor, in the new fashion, bluntly indicated to him. All of the treatment was directed at control of pain, enhancing mobility and delaying inevitable death. Maximum life expectancy? Two years would be an optimistic appraisal.

It was the waste, as well as the pain, that tore Moss's

personal defenses apart. The loss of potential was outrageous. There was too much in that boy to be buried unfulfilled. He had arrived at manhood too late to be deprived of it so early. The childhood disease was claiming the inner child before the outer man had even the smallest measure of life. And the pain, the constant pain, he could almost feel it himself. He had begun to dread Adam's visits and yet Adam was with him, intruding on every other patient's hour, intruding and dominating his private life, intruding even into his own dreams.

Moss's thoughts were interrupted by the somber tone as much as the fact of Adam's next statements.

"I'm not going to analyze this dream, Doctor. I'm not going to analyze any dreams any more. It's really too late for all of that. It's become a game."

"It's up to you, Adam."

He had stopped using the last-name formalism which was part of his traditional conduct towards all patients. But then, how long had it been since he had considered this anything approaching an analytic treatment? What was he doing for the boy? Supporting, comforting, perhaps sharing, but certainly not psychoanalyzing and not even counseling. What was there to counsel?

"I don't need your help for living now. The only thing you can really do for me now, is to help me die. I cannot stand it any more. I cannot stand the pain. I don't like what it's doing to me. I don't like what it's making me do to Sarah. I'm not afraid to die, Doctor, at least I don't think I am. I'm afraid to die *wrong*. I'm afraid of the disgusting thing I might become. I won't do that. Not to anybody; not to my sisters, my mother, my father and certainly not to Sarah. You've got to help me."

"I don't know what you mean, Adam," lied Peter Moss, knowing only too well what he meant.

"Do you know of Percy Bridgeman?" Adam asked.

"You mean Bridgeman, the Harvard philosopher?"

"No, I mean Bridgeman, the former Harvard physicist," Adam repsonded with humor, reclaiming Bridgeman for his own.

"Do you know how he died, Doctor?"

"I'm afraid I don't."

"Well, this noble and wise man, this physicist, philosopher, teacher, with the inequity that the religious in their stupidity attribute to 'God's way'—was cursed with some damn deteriorative and degenerative disease. He watched himself slowly diminish in powers, in capacities, aware of the fact that he would soon be reduced to a passive vegetable and that all control of his own estate would pass from his volition. His speech was going, his sight was going, his ambulation was going. He waited until he sensed mobility was too painful, too exhausting, and command over his life was slipping from his hands. Then, with the last steps he could manage, he dragged his dying body from his house to his garage, where he took a shotgun that he had prepared for just this appropriate moment and, using the last reservoir of courage, strength, stamina and intelligence, he blew his head off. At least, so I have been told.

"I want to die like Percy Bridgeman. I don't necessarily mean with a shotgun. But I want to die at a moment, not in pieces. I want to die as a decision, not as an instrument of the decisions of others. I want to die purposefully, with active intention. If you want to know the truth, what I really would want to do is die in an act of glory, but those days are over. I don't suppose I can volunteer in some dangerous psychoanalytic research you're involved in? To sacrifice myself for science? Can I?"

Peter Moss laughed because he knew that was what Adam wanted. At that same moment he became aware that despite what he might now say, when the time came he would supply Adam with the means for at least a quick, if not a glorious, end.

"If only there were causes to die for," Adam said.

"If only there were dragons to slay, you mean," echoed Moss, reverting to an analytic interpretation to conclude the hour.

Chapter I

September—twenty-two months before the convention

The whole arrangement had the trappings of a Grade B movie and Lowell Stoneham did not like it one bit. What the hell kind of place was that for a meeting anyway? Montauk! he thought with a shudder of distaste. Some God-forsaken middle-class resort at the end of the world. Why not Coney Island or Atlantic City? Obviously the desire for anonymity had dictated the selection of a locale other than the traditional meeting places of such a group—a place less likely to attract attention; where men of their stature might go unrecognized, but surely some consideration could have been shown to common convenience and taste.

Who will be there? Stoneham wondered as he suddenly became aware that he really did not know. He smiled, amazed at how much he had taken on faith because the invitation had come from Admiral Mudd. Damn that man, he thought, the power he holds over people, including me! Will I ever stop feeling like a schoolboy in his presence?

The request had stated that he come to the Montauk Yacht Club—whatever the hell that was—with a maximum of discretion and an attempt at total anonymity. He was told to come alone. Nonetheless, it had been twenty years since Lowell Stoneham had driven a car and he was not about to start now. The concession he made was discomforting enough, sitting in the front seat of a Hertz Chevrolet, almost shoulder to shoulder with his own chauffeur. A younger Stoneham might have found it amusing but at sixty-five, there were few concessions of comfort that he was prepared to make for entertainment. He and the chauffeur, in a ridiculous attempt to establish a cover of collegiality, had independently managed to discover the same "disguise." They ended up being dressed almost exactly the same in Lacoste shirts and lightweight flannel golf slacks. It was hard to tell who was made more uncomfortable by the experience.

Stoneham wondered if he had ever in his life been to Montauk. He doubted it. He disliked public places in general and Long Island in particular. Those few trips that were mandated to Long Island inevitably involved family obligations at his brother's Manhasset estate. As the car moved off Route 111 onto the coastal road, however, Stoneham began to recognize familiar sights. The windmill in East Hampton reminded him that in his politically more active days, he had maintained membership in a beach club there. At most he had attended a few luncheons—always on the pressure of soliciting votes or funds or simply to soothe inflated egos. He smiled as he thought of the distinctions made by the "upwardly mobile." Public places are all the same and all offensive, he thought.

Lowell Stoneham had now reached the age where he allowed few demands to be made upon him. Always a private man, he was uncomfortable with those not of his immediate background, and the feigned camaraderie demanded by the political life was an unremitting burden. The eldest of the Stoneham brothers had now done his service and felt entitled to retreat into the privacy he had always desired.

The Stoneham children had been raised with a constant awareness of the immense Stoneham fortune. It was his father, in particular, who had felt that such enormous wealth demanded service to avoid corruption. A disreputable and despised robber baron great-grandfather who had made a fortune in steel and railroads, had lived to see his grandson, Lowell's father, compound that fortune with respectability by the immense amalgamation which occurred when he married Mary Hardweg Melton, sole heiress to the vast fortune of the Pennsylvania Melton banking empire. Raised in the privacy of wealth and privilege, the Stoneham sons were encouraged to public service, and none had answered that call more diligently than the eldest, Lowell. Assistant Secretary of Defense under Eisenhower, adviser to Presidents, four-term Governor of the Commonwealth of Pennsylvania, Lowell Stoneham had three times sought the nomination for the presidency of the United States, and—despite his obvious entitlement and despite the general acknowledgment that he probably would have been an outstanding President—Lowell Stoneham had seen the nomination denied him on all three attempts; on one occasion at least, for reasons so trivial as to border on humiliation.

He had been disciplined to be a good soldier, and gracious acceptance of defeat was a necessary part of the code of those who rarely suffer defeat. He had managed to avoid bitterness until the wretched maneuvering of Roger Hilton deprived him of the nomination for the final time. When Hilton became President, Lowell Stoneham retired from active politics. Only later was he to appreciate the irony that this final disappointment and bitterness had, perversely, allowed him to ascend to new power in the party during the seven years since The Scandal. His open split with Hilton, his obvious contempt for the man, had made him an heroic figure, one of the few left in the party. In addition, he now had the power of a man who needs nothing more of anyone and who wants nothing he cannot himself supply.

No one commanded Lowell Stoneham. No one, that was, except, perhaps, Admiral Horace Mudd. What was it in the character and person of Mudd that demanded allegiance, that commanded obedience? Perhaps it was that he never seemed to use his authority; he never seemed to issue orders. His gentle requests were simply treated as commands by everyone. And with Stoneham, there was the special relationship of a shared past. Stoneham had first met Mudd when as a young man barely out of Princeton he enlisted in the navy; was commissioned an Ensign, and met the already impressive Commander Mudd at a reception at the Forrestals'. Not yet the distinguished war hero, he was nonetheless a commanding presence. One sensed his iron self-discipline which seemed enhanced by an old-fashioned sense of manners that bordered on courtliness; beyond everything else, he projected an aura of absolute and unquestionable integrity.

Stoneham always felt awkward and adolescent in the presence of Mudd. There was something in Mudd that managed to make him feel ill-kempt, gauche and inept. Perhaps there were qualities in Mudd that reminded Lowell of his father; and, indeed, Mudd treated him paternally but never in a patronizing way. Stoneham smiled to himself. How do things like that happen? he wondered. Mudd couldn't be more than eight or ten years his senior, yet he always sensed a rush of self-conscious apprehension and excitement when Mudd contacted him. In his presence, he was always the little boy awaiting either approval or chastisement. He wondered if he had ever made it to the presidency, would that have altered the relationship between the Admiral and himself? He tended to doubt it.

The meeting had been set up five weeks before, and he still had no ideas as to its purpose, nor was he even sure who would be there. The car continued on its measured course at a constant and unaltered fifty-five miles an hour down the Montauk Highway. Stoneham had flown in from Seal Harbor to Manhasset, stopped for lunch at his brother's estate, where he had arranged for his chauffeur to arrive with a rented car. Now that they were approaching the semi-private, semi-public marina where the meeting had been scheduled, he wished to get on with the business as rapidly as possible and get back to his private world, where things were controlled, known, predictable, and as they should be. Since he had given up all aspiration for public office, or more accurately, since age had defeated his purposes, he now found himself more powerful than ever, more sought after, more courted. He had nothing more to ask, and everything to give—immense wealth, the power that may or may not always go with it, and credentials of a lifetime of service in politics, compounded by the general guilt felt within the ranks for having frustrated him in the one goal he had wanted and, by almost every standard, deserved. He would do this one last service to the party and then insist they leave him alone, to his own affairs.

As the car pulled into the vast marina a slight grimace of distaste crossed his face. What was there about the place that seemed so tacky? The parking lot had more than its share of white Mercedes and large Cadillac sedans. Yet, despite that—or was it because of that?—it seemed seedy, parvenu and distasteful. The chauffeur parked the car and, unconsciously, walked around to open the door, as Stoneham, just as mechanically, waited for it to be opened. To an observer the scene had to seem ludicrous, given their dress, car and locale.

Stoneham headed out toward the docks. The chauffeur settled himself on a bench along the edge of the parking lot with a thermos of iced coffee, an Agatha Christie mystery and a copy of the *Wall Street Journal*. He was a man interested in finance and used to waiting.

As Stoneham turned the corner of the quay, the rows of docks beyond the large marina store and service station came into sight. The literally hundreds of boats parked cheek by jowl looked like tenements, belying the amount of money invested in their purchase, care and maintenance. As he came to the most distant dock, following the telephoned instructions, he walked past dozens of seemingly identical (at least to the uninitiated) tuna fishing boats with their awkward bridges and clumsy scaffoldings. When he turned the corner into the last dock, Stoneham immediately spotted the *Five Star Final*. What made this fifty-three-foot Rybovitch stand out like a diamond in a bracelet of paste stones? Was it his knowledge of how much it cost, or simply a lifetime of exposure to the expensive and handcrafted which made him sensitive to the differences?

The *Five Star Final* was not, as one might have expected from its name, the property of a newspaperman. When Horace Mudd had graduated as an ensign from Annapolis his wedding present from his wife had been a small sailing dinghy on which she had emblazoned, with only half irony, the pentagon of five stars that was the mark of the senior admiral or general in the military services. He had risen rapidly in the Naval Air Force during World War II, a rapidity that offended many of the conservative battleship warriors. Despite this unparalleled success, his extraordinary brilliance, reserve and integrity had managed to keep his enemies to a minimum. And when in the waning days of the Korean War, despite all odds, at age forty-six, he had been named by Harry Truman a five-star admiral, it was greeted with incredulity (none, after all, had been created since World War II and no one expected any) but without great resistance.

His rise in life had been accompanied by a succession of ever larger boats named *Five Star I, II, III*. Finally, after the death of his wife and his retirement from active government service, he had bought the boat on which he intended to spend the declining years of his life in retirement. The name, suitably, was *Five Star Final*.

The cabin shades were drawn and at the dock, greeting arrivals, was Grundy, an ex-CPO with a badly burned neck and face who had been in the Admiral's service since his first command in World War II. Word had it the scars were the result of a fire aboard ship in which Grundy had saved the then Lieutenant Commander Mudd's life. It was typical of Horace Mudd that such romantic rumors would arise, and also that the man's reserve allowed no one to question him about the validity of the story.

"They're waiting for you, sir," Grundy said with his seaman's manners as he offered a hand to help Stoneham aboard the boat.

Stoneham walked into the small cabin and noticed there were six people already seated around a crowded table.

"Lowell, good of you to come."

That remark was spoken in a soft voice still carrying the edge of the accent of the West Virginia hills he had left over forty years before. Courteous, soft-spoken, never known to have lost his temper in front of anyone, Mudd commanded the kind of authority on the multiple boards of business and philanthropic organizations on which he served, that he had in the former days of the navy. If ever a man was a natural leader—if ever that term had true relevance—it was in relationship to Horace Mudd.

The structure of The Establishment was loose, never precisely defined, but it existed nonetheless, and Horace Mudd, a former five-star admiral, a former Secretary of Defense, a former head of the World Bank, was the acknowledged leader of The Establishment. It was not by chance that he was chairing this meeting.

"I think you know everyone here, at least by name," the Admiral continued with a slight smile.

Sitting to the right of the Admiral was Senator John Wentworth.

"How the hell are you, Jack?" Stoneham said, grabbing his right hand between both of his hands.

John Wentworth, Senate Minority Leader, had been a Senator from Illinois for sixteen years and was the eldest son of the Wentworth family which had endowed the Wentworth Bank, the Wentworth Foundation, the Wentworth Fellowships, and represented one of the largest privately held fortunes in the United States. It was built on, of all things, the slick conversion by traditional grain merchants into the packaging of cattle foods, and from there into pet food and even a cereal—almost indistinguishable in form from their dog biscuits—meant for human consumption. John Wentworth had the kind of looks that when stripped of his position and official trappings, made him automatically disappear in a crowd. He did, nonetheless, look distinctly out of character now in a Hawaiian print shirt (where on earth had he got it?), baseball cap and dark glasses. No one had remembered ever seeing John Wentworth in public without a white shirt, conservative tie and gray—always gray—suit. This was then his ultimate sacrifice to the Admiral's request for anonymity.

Next to him was Jimmy Saperstein, a man of little direct power, but obviously a representative of the Press at this meeting. James Saperstein had been a PR hack for years and carried with him the mentality and vocabulary of a promotion man. When the Washington *Post* decided that, for purposes of image, it was essential to have a conservative columnist on their editorial pages it toyed with the obvious choice of William Buckley, deciding reluctantly that the dangers of so brilliant a spokesman for an opposing position outweighed the cachet his column might have given their editorial pages. They settled, therefore, for James Saperstein, who had managed to escape the Hilton administration and The Scandal relatively unscathed. To everyone's surprise, Jimmy Saperstein's column became an enormously popular and influential part of the journalism scene. Syndication, and a buy-out by Tom Whiting, head of the Los Angeles *News* chain, made him a force in public opinion, and the leading spokesman for the conservative views of his boss, a key member of The Establishment. More important than that, Jimmy Saperstein was a party man, used to taking orders, and ready to take on organizational tasks which a Tom Whiting would not be free to. He was there as Tom Whiting's "boy." His physical appearance was, by design, a total denial of his background. He had literally modeled himself after images he had collected of proper English gentlemen. All his clothes were bespoken from shops on Jermyn Street or Savile Row—shops whose names he had culled over the years from English gentry he had met. One year on assignment in England had even left traces of a British accent. His winter trademark was a precise inch of white cuff which always managed to extend beyond his jackets—just barely exposing the edge of a flat, discreet gold disc cuff link. Confounded by the anonymity and casualness of the occasion—left, in other words, to the impromptu devices of his own taste—the image had fallen apart. Lightweight gray flannel slacks were fine with the white Swiss linen shirt rolled to above the elbows—but the conceit was betrayed by an alligator belt and a pair of leather slip-ons (worn without socks, of course), both vulgarly marked with the Gucci trademark.

Stephen Cross, senior partner of the distinguished and influential Wall Street law firm of Hardman, Cross and Lowenstein, was a trustee of Yale, on the Boards of the Ford Foundation and Council for Foreign Affairs and Chairman of the Board of the Metropolitan Museum. He had a talent for raising money unmatched by any other man in the United States, both through prestigious clients of his law firm and his family connections, his wife being an heiress to the O'Keefe lumber fortune. He was, himself, a boatman partial to power. He had driven his *Cigarette* over from the Southampton Beach Club—and docked at a respectable distance from the point of assignation. A tall, lean man, his face, though tanned, still showed peel marks on his forehead and the bridge of his nose, from hours of recent exposure on the water. He was wearing a sweat shirt, light blue jeans stained from years of mechanical tinkering, and an old pair of Sperry Top Siders. His sandy hair was cut in an unfashionable bristle and he needed a shave. His eyes were flinty blue—but the long narrow shape and habitual squint of the outdoorsman exposed little iris. It was an ideal face for a poker player—a game at which he excelled. His passion, however, was bridge—and while a high-stakes club player, he could never make top rank in the bridge world because of an essential insensitivity for partner communication. It had cost him a considerable amount of money trying.

The one woman at the table seemed strikingly out of place. First, the fact that she was a woman; and secondly, she was at least twenty years younger than anyone else seated at the table. Kate Parr, elegant, beautiful and severe-looking; black hair cut in a Prince Valiant style; suit tailored to the kind of perfection one doesn't usually associate with women's clothes; and with a composure that rivaled that of the Admiral himself. Kate Parr was Lincoln McAllister's right-hand "man." She spoke for him; she represented him; she was his complete confidante; and everyone who knew the junior Senator from New York treated her, Kate Parr, as his absolute surrogate. It was generally assumed that she was his lover. She was not. Not that she would have denied Lincoln McAllister even that—she was one of those people passionately devoted to the person she served—she would have denied him nothing. Fortunately, he made no such demands on her.

Lincoln McAllister, despite the kind of extraordinary good looks that are usually reserved for an occasional movie star or for illustrations in magazines, was an old-fashioned moralist, a devoted husband and committed family man. Although he had the "sex appeal" that made him an inevitably appealing person to both sexes, he was not essentially or excessively a sexual person. Besides, Kate Parr was a confirmed lesbian.

Her presence in the group was essential, since one of the key actors in the meeting was Lincoln McAllister. Two months previously, at a high-level meeting of a broad representation of The Establishment it had been decided that Lincoln McAllister was to be the party nominee for President in the next election. It was part of the grooming process that he be carefully protected and isolated during the crucial period before he would "emerge" as, first, a logical and, then, inevitable candidate.

Lowell Stoneham looked at the sixth man at the table, annoyed with himself for not remembering the name of that vaguely familiar face. Not that the face was one to remember or, indeed, meant to be remembered, yet, damn it, Stoneham thought, he is someone to be remembered.

His train of thought was interrupted by Admiral Mudd saying: "Gentlemen." Kate Parr smiled at the form of address. Rather than taking umbrage she wisely acknowledged it was the ultimate sign of her acceptance. "I know you must be somewhat puzzled at my urgently convening the session so shortly after our Bohemia Club meeting, but we have come to a major conclusion which will need your approval and support. I apologize for the inconveniences we may have caused you, and I am personally grateful for your co-operation. Having said that, let me now simply turn the meeting over to Hugh Baker, whom you all know."

Of course, Stoneham thought, that's who it is! Hugh Baker—a shadowy figure in the bureaucracy of Intelligence, originally an aide to Horace Mudd, but now a power in his own right. His name was readily recognizable only to members of The Establishment and instantly recognizable to all of them. Hugh Baker was fifty-three years old, with a boyish look that despite his age was only now just beginning to fade. His blondish hair was turning gray and the steel-rimmed glasses he had worn since his twenties were beginning to have the look of granny glasses although they had formerly given him the look of a precocious child.

And a precocious young child was what he had been. Baker, descendant of five generations of Congregationalist ministers in Framingham, Massachusetts, had been a sixteen-year-old Japanese language major at Harvard College at the outbreak of World War II. Swept into the cryptography unit set up by Edwin Reischauer to break the Japanese Code, he had quickly come to the attention of Horace Mudd. Highly neurotic as a young boy in college, unstable, with a tendency towards alcoholism and gambling, he had subsequently settled down to do brilliant work in Naval Intelligence, and then as soon as the war was over immediately began to fall apart again.

With marriage, however, he began to restabilize. He gave up drinking, and settled into academia, eventually becoming a professor of Far Eastern languages at Georgetown University. Shortly after his marriage, when it had become apparent that his emotional life was in order, he was contacted by Mudd and recruited for the CIA. In the beginning his academic life was allowed a primary focus, but within a few years he was a full-time key figure in Intelligence. The academic appointment was a convenient cover, particularly since Baker maintained his scholastic credentials by continuing his research, albeit part-time. While he was actively involved with the CIA, he was marked as The Establishment's representative in the Intelligence community, and would be rotated to satisfy particular needs. Throughout his career he maintained this dual role, taking leaves of absence from the university throughout the party's administrations to perform critical functions, often publicly ill defined and usually officially attached to the Department of Defense, Treasury or Commerce—whichever seemed most discreet.

Under the Hilton administration there had been strong pressure from the White House to name him

Director of the CIA. With the bulldoggedness and arrogance that Roger Hilton consistently displayed toward those who had built the party and would have to support it after he had made a shambles of it, he almost won his point. It took the direct intervention of Horace Mudd to convince the then President Hilton that it was imperative that Hugh Baker be kept out of the public limelight and shielded from public criticism. Whoever was named the head of the CIA, the real power would still be Hugh Baker, based not on title—but on the recognition of his special relationship to The Establishment. And, indeed, he was the power. The decision to shield Baker proved itself a brilliant one only too quickly. While the public exposures that were the fallout from the then unexpected scandals destroyed careers at a wholesale level, Baker survived.

Hugh Baker leaned slightly forward and began to address the group. "Ms. Parr and gentlemen," he started, with a tacit and dry dig at the Admiral's original address. "You are, I am afraid, not going to like what follows. Nor do we. But we have examined all other options and have reluctantly decided that the course we are recommending is the only viable one. The facts are simple; the time is short; and the decision seems inevitable.

"We have in Lincoln McAllister an obvious candidate who in normal times would be an odds-on favorite to run away with the election. He should be President. He would make a fine President. And he is young enough so he could be the cornerstone for rebuilding the mess that has come to be the party. In our estimation we will never have a better chance than we do today, with as weak a leader as is now in the White House, and with as attractive a candidate as Link. We have an ideal situation and we must win this coming election. Normally we would all be jubilant. But the most meticulous studies indicate beyond any doubt that even with the 'ideal situation'—in the wake of The Scandal it will still be impossible to elect our candidate."

"Damn that man. That truly evil man," John Wentworth muttered, shaking his head softly. To this day the thought of The Scandal horrified him. He was the least devious of those sitting around the table, and the one who could have been said to be the most morally offended by Hilton.

The Scandal had almost shattered the country. For years it had been known that both parties had been influencing the primaries of the opposition parties. No one, however, had carried it to the point of its corruptly logical extreme. It remained for Hilton to go beyond *influencing*—to actual choosing of the weakest opposition candidate via selective elimination of the stronger candidates. The plans included faked evidence, forged letters, planted stories and in at least one documented case, blackmail.

With the shocking suicide of Senator Ralph Hoffman, the extent of the manipulations became public. The exposure was generally tolerated by the country at large with an unexpected calm. The cynicism that pervaded the entire national political scene; the traditional American respect for a winner; and the natural reverence with which the public endowed the presidency allowed Hilton to ride out the original protests. And in the beginning the protests were ridiculously subdued; after all, it was still short of buying the election.

Only after the Blue Memoranda had been discovered and published did public outrage begin to reach threatening levels. Written on blue paper, with blue ink to discourage copies, they were in the President's own handwriting. They outlined an ingenious plan labeled "Dominocus" which would have effectively suspended all national elections in the United States, but unlike the traditional South American-style coups by a man-on-the-white-horse, Dominocus was purebred Madison Avenue. There would be no need for a military coup, because elections would "seem to be" held. People would go to the polls, pull their levers, wait in suspense, until the predesignated candidates would eventually be announced. Manipulation of the primaries and control of the computer bases would maintain an illusion of the democratic process. The plan was even extended to allow for future victories of candidates labeled as members of the opposing party. The testimony of the "experts" on handwriting managed for a while to obfuscate as much as possible the question of the validity of the documents and to blunt criticism until the amazing exposure of a *second* diary of the President's. Here in great detail, and with incredible indiscretion, he discussed the writing of the memoranda, thus confirming beyond even a shadow of a doubt his authorship. It would later emerge that the plan had already been tested in three state elections and had aroused no suspicion.

To this day no one was sure whether Dominocus would have been taken with as much seriousness as it ought to have been. After all, it was then still considered "theoretical" and the theoretical can be cast as metaphor. It was another game plan and plans are not always intended to be implemented. What truly aroused the population was the exposure of a backup plan devised by senior staff officers for military seizure of the government if for one reason or another Dominocus did not work. It was a pure example of the kind of stupid and foolish overkill that characterizes the military mentality. It was contrary to the whole principle of the Blue Memoranda, which by avoiding the appearance of implementation by force maintained the illusion of freedom.

Despite the rapid indictment of two members of the Joint Chiefs of Staff by the Justice Department the military documents terrified and outraged the public, and sealed Hilton's fate.

Hilton persisted in denying knowledge of the military backup plan. To this day there is a strong feeling by those in the Administration that he might indeed have been uninvolved in it. He continued to deny Dominocus, claiming that the Blue Memoranda were merely theoretical extensions of a "promotional concept." Serious academic arguments were brought forward on the distinction between education, persuasion and brainwashing. It was generally conceded that Hilton could indeed have survived had it not been for the stupidity of the two generals.

Wentworth shook himself out of reverie, aware that Baker was continuing.

"No candidate from our party can run for national office and expect to win with Roger Hilton as an albatross around his neck. If we wait for normal attrition we estimate it will be another twenty-five years before The Scandal will be sufficiently defused so that we will be able to move into office. By that time, gentlemen, there will be no party. We must confront the problem of Roger Hilton."

"What are we supposed to do? Shoot the cocksucker?" interjected Lowell Stoneham with a venomous contempt that he felt for the ex-President who, beyond betraying his country and his party, had in addition personally denied him his final opportunity for the presidency.

"For God's sake, Lowell, watch your language. There's a woman present," cautioned John Wentworth with obvious discomfort.

Kate Parr smiled. There was something attractive about old-fashioned manners and old-fashioned ways.

"Rather than shooting the—albatross," Baker continued, "we had thought of resurrecting him."

"The last resurrection required divine power," Kate Parr amusedly offered. "Have you arranged for that, Mr. Baker?"

"I'm afraid," Baker continued professorially, "our efforts will have to be superhuman rather than supra, but then, who knows whether there is really a distinction?"

"For us simple folk," Saperstein said, "would you explain what you mean by 'resurrection'?"

Saperstein was given to using the kind of self-deprecating remarks that intimated a superiority which allows for that privilege.

"We have decided," Baker continued, "that no presidential candidate can be elected carrying on his back someone like Roger Hilton. The only conceivable solution is to convert Roger Hilton from a villain into a hero once again. We have a little over two years to do it. And we think we can."

"Well, I suppose if we can convert garbage into compost in one season," said John Wentworth, "in two years we ought to be able to do the human equivalent."

"Garbage isn't shit," said Stoneham. "And compost isn't gold. And if there were such an alchemist, he'd have been working for my family years ago."

"I concede that it is not going to be easy," continued Baker in his professorial dry manner. "But we think it can be done."

The understatement carried with it the group's knowledge of the man and his reputation. Baker did not speculate; he planned. When he said, "We think it can be done," that meant that meticulous studies indicated the project could succeed.

Baker then outlined the thinking that had gone on between the two meetings. The campaign for McAllister for the nomination was no problem at all. Indeed, the whole agenda for the election, following the nomination, seemed almost too promising. At each phase, however, the figure of Roger Hilton emerged like an ugly yellow smear. It then became apparent that image had to be erased from this campaign, and from all future campaigns. The Republican Party had suffered from the image of Hoover for over twenty-five years and in the end, only age, patience and time had lent respectability to that name. But their party could not now afford twenty-five years. They had to move and move quickly.

Baker listed some of the advantages already present. All of the major figures imprisoned in The Scandal were now out of prison or on their way out. The books they had written, having hit the best-seller lists, were now out of the bookstores and out of the news. The publicity was beginning to abate. Hilton, himself, was getting older. HIs wife, always a pathetic figure, was an asset which could be exploited. His son had left his job with the Fluor Corporation and had enrolled in New York Theological Seminary. He would shortly be ordained as an Episcopal priest. His daughter was now pregnant and the typical pictures of the proud grandfather would add the appropriate softening touch. Besides, there was always that hard core of the public who would continue to see Hilton as a victim of the left-wing press.

Baker then proceeded to outline the campaign in all of its meticulous detail, and while intricate, it was not complicated. It involved the traditional media blitz, and required the active utilization of the sympathetic powers in the academic community, the political community and the press and television. The key figures in all areas had already been identified and while some resistance might be encountered most, with the possible exception of a few key figures in Congress, could be expected to go along. The congressional leadership would admittedly be difficult, but Baker was confident they could be handled.

"How in hell are you going to pull that off?" Saperstein asked. "You'll need at least the tacit co-operation of the Democratic leadership as well as ours, and I'm not sure he doesn't have as many enemies in the latter as the former."

"We're confident we can work that out," Baker said with an almost ominous dryness in his voice.

Stephen Cross looked up at the last statement and said, "I want to know precisely what that means."

At this point Admiral Mudd interrupted, saying, "Gentlemen, can we allow some details on faith? If Hugh has to define all of the contingencies we have allowed for—we may be here for the entire weekend."

Cross was annoyed—and alerted. As a lawyer he knew that the details, the "contingencies," were often the make-or-break points—and he did not like to be left unaware. Still, his role was a particularly critical one, and he had been determined to be as inconspicuous as possible at the meeting. He quickly withdrew into silence—regretting his impulsive statement.

Baker then continued to outline the plan, which involved gradually increasing appearances on public television; arrangements for speeches in the academic community; honorary degrees; appointments to the boards of philanthropic organizations; the beginning of invitations to significant artistic and philanthropic functions—all meticulously nonpolitical and all accompanied by pre-written statements given to Hilton for memorization. They were going to take no chance on the Hilton paranoid arrogance. A subtle media blitz would accompany the increased public appearances, all supported by "wise and temperate" statements attributed to Hilton. The Soviet bribery cases with which the Democratic Party was now involved would be played up, and, in a teeter-totter effect, The Scandal would begin to seem less significant or unique.

The discussion continued for another hour and a half, going progressively into more detail. The group began to appreciate the care that had gone into its planning, and with that, the feasibility of its success.

"I still don't like it," Stoneham said. "I don't see why we should have to do anything for that piece of dirt."

"We're not doing it for him, Lowell, we're doing it for Lincoln McAllister and the party," said John Wentworth, now firmly convinced of its wisdom.

"Precisely," said Horace Mudd.

Through it all Kate Parr had remained silent. She had been shocked at some of the suggestions, incredulous at the care and extent of the planning, and while generally approving, she remained troubled. The plan, of course, demanded the co-operation of Lincoln McAllister. She, alone, knew the intensity of McAllister's hatred for Roger Hilton. Lincoln was not a man of strong passions. Despite his sensual looks and the roguish image that had been cultivated, he was a careful, conservative, fastidious, almost obsessional person who rarely allowed emotions to overrule his sense of balance, propriety and order. The one area—and the only area—in which Kate Parr had seen him emotional was where Hilton was concerned. He was monomaniacal on the subject, with an icy hatred that went beyond reasoning.

Fifteen minutes into Baker's presentation, she had been convinced of the wisdom of his decision. She had heard much of Baker, had never met him, and she was in awe of the computerlike nature of his reasoning, presentation and work. It would work. And, of course, he was right. McAllister must be President! Given that, all that followed was inevitable, and proper. The question was, could she guarantee that Lincoln McAllister would acquiesce? She would have to make it her business to see that he did. Her thoughts were interrupted, almost as if read, by the Admiral.

"Miss Parr," he said with a certain intensity, "Lincoln will understand the necessity for this operation and co-operate."

Was it a question or a command? she wondered. With Horace Mudd it was wise to assume the latter.

"He will co-operate," she said simply with an outer assurance that masked her inner disquiet.

"Only one thing, Admiral," Saperstein asked, "what about RH? I presume he has been apprised."

Stoneham snorted his contempt. My God, he thought, the mere announcement of cosmetic surgery was sufficient to make an unreconstructed sycophant like Jimmy Saperstein revert to the "RH" address associated with Hilton at his peak of power. Damn it, thought Stoneham, those bastards know their game. It will work. It will *really* work. It's begun to work already!

"Mr. Hilton has been consulted and told what he must do," the Admiral said. The mild emphasis on the word *told* and the slight edge in his voice when he said Mr. Hilton indicated to the group that Mudd's feeling about Roger Hilton remained unchanged, and never for a moment had been allowed to be a factor in the decision that had to be made.

"You gentlemen," Mudd continued, "will of course not communicate with Hilton directly. We will leave that all in the competent hands of Hugh Baker. All the liaison will be carried out through Jim Doyle."

With the mention of Doyle's name a slight murmur went through the small group. Doyle, perhaps the most loved and in many ways the most tragic—certainly the most tragic—figure in the Hilton administration, out of some perverse sense of personal loyalty had stayed with the ex-President during his years of exile. No one quite understood what could have kept him in that bind except a depth of affection bordering on love. And since no one could conceive of anyone loving Roger Hilton, Jim Doyle had become a mysterious and ambiguous, if not totally tragic, figure.

"Hugh and I had decided that at this first meeting

it would be best to keep Doyle out, until we were convinced that all of you concurred with the plan. One hopes we will not have to risk another summit conference this large. Small group meetings attract less attention and, after all, we are all old friends. But you ought to know that Jim Doyle is to be considered a full member of the team and privy to all our decisions.

"If there are no more questions, then, gentlemen," the Admiral continued, standing, "I suggest the meeting is over. We have our work to do."

And with no more than a few handshakes the group began to disperse. As Stephen Cross was making his personal farewells the Admiral stared at him intently, saying:

"Was there something you wished to say privately, Stephen?"

"No, sir. What made you ask?"

"You seemed uncharacteristically quiet."

"I was 'uncharacteristically' in absolute accordance with what was being proposed. I fully approve, Admiral."

"I depend on that, Stephen. I depend on your full cooperation."

"Of course you know you will have it—now as always."

"I haven't seen much of you lately, Stephen; we must get together more socially."

"I would like that, sir; and so would Emily."

"Yes, I have been too reclusive lately. One loses touch. Do give your lovely wife my fond regards."

The chauffeur, alerted by that particular sensitivity of longtime servants, put away his paperback (the newspaper had long since been discarded) and capped his thermos only moments before he heard the familiar steps of his employer. He opened the front right door of the Chevy, but this time Stoneham entered the back seat. He had made enough concessions of comfort for one day. As the car proceeded to retrace its tracks back along the Montauk Highway, he was aware of the fact that he had not been offered a drink aboard, and that he wanted one. Now with annoyance he remembered that he was not in his own car, and there was, of course, no bar in the rented car. Lowell Stoneham was not a heavy drinker, and he recognized his desire for a drink as a signal of some vague anxiety. Something didn't sit right. The logic was there—but to a man his age, instinct was more important, and he didn't like the way he was feeling.

Enough of this cloak-and-dagger bullshit, he thought. It's not my game, not any more, he thought, and to his driver he said,

"When we get to East Hampton, stop at the Maidstone," suddenly remembering the name of the club.

Chapter II

September—twenty-two months before the convention

Letter from Stephen Cross to Roger Hilton

Dear Roger,

Prepare for your second coming. They have swallowed the bait, and, indeed, with a nice kind of irony have decided to call the operation Red Herring. I have decided, in my own mind, to label our version of the operation Killer Whale.

They have no suspicion what kind of fish they have on their line, and by the time they do, it will be too late. There was the resistance we anticipated from Stoneham, but as would be expected, he deferred to Horace Mudd.

Kate Parr was unusually quiet. I would have thought McAllister had everything to gain and nothing to lose. She is too good a poker player to show anything. There was no sense of elation, of victory. At this point all she knows is what the others know; that you are to be passively restored to public graces and then quietly tucked away in a ceremonial position. Why no enthusiasm? Is there something about McAllister that I don't know? I'm worried that he may give us trouble.

STEPHEN

Letter from Roger Hilton to Stephen Cross

Dear Steve:

Congratulations on the successful launching of Operation Killer Whale. Do not worry about McAllister. There is nothing you need to know. I got a lasso around his balls and he knows it. Believe me, there will be no problems there.

RH

Cross reread the letter for the third time. What the hell did that all mean? McAllister came out of The Scandal clean as a whistle. One of the few people who was almost converted into a hero. He had always maintained a distance from Hilton, and in the end had left the Administration on principle and well before the debacle. In addition, everyone was aware of his personal distaste for Hilton. In a more emotional man one would have said hatred, but with the cool McAllister one didn't think of those words. What was up? Roger Hilton never showed anyone his whole hand. Something was missing. Stephen Cross didn't like it.

Chapter III

November—twenty months before the convention

> Mrs. Roger Hilton made her first public appearance since her recent illness when she addressed the Greater Charleston Fund's dinner last night. (November 10, Charleston *Post*)

Sarah poured the heavily steeped English breakfast tea into a fine Japanese porcelain cup. The tea was Adam's favorite and he drank it day and night. He enjoyed the hot tea in old-fashioned, heavy pottery mugs, but the weight of the pottery with eight ounces of tea had begun to become noticeably difficult for him to handle, so she had bought the delicate porcelain tea service under a pretext that neither fooled him nor herself. She stirred in a half teaspoon of sugar and a dollop of milk and brought it to Adam, who was lying propped up in the bed. He had found that the pain could be best controlled in two different ways. One was in the hammock that he had devised for the bathtub which supported his body away from the enamel tub and permitted him almost to float in the warm water. The other place of comfort was on the bed with a special backrest he had devised, and with down pillows propped under his knees.

He was lying there in bed now, hardly acknowledging Sarah's coming and going, deeply absorbed in his current readings. Sarah would have preferred being ignorant of the subject of his current "research" but she was only too aware. For months now he had been studying toxicology and pharmacology and she knew he was planning the most convenient and least offensive means of killing himself. She returned to the kitchen to clear the remnants of the light supper they had had and quickly lit a cigarette. On Adam's urging she had given up cigarettes when they had first met, but started smoking again shortly after the onset of his illness. She never smoked in his presence and pretended that she was still off cigarettes. He in turn pretended not to know she had returned to smoking. It was a reasonable arrangement. It kept her smoking down, and the furtiveness and secretiveness about smoking became a displacement for all of the essential duplicity necessary to avoid the constant subject of death. They pretended, when possible, that death did not exist, in order to avoid the total domination of their thoughts and their conversation in that small portion of life which remained for the two of them.

Adam continually repeated that it was not death, but the dying that bothered him. For Sarah it was more complicated. She was not so sure for herself. The agonies of his dying, even with the anticipation of increasing pain, were a torture she thought she could survive. She did not, however, know if she could endure his death. The fact that this so young man, this boy, this baby, her lover, her child, would soon simply not be, was unacceptable, unendurable. She could not bear the thought of his termination, of his ceasing to be before he had been. Where would she go without him; where had she been before him?

Sarah Pedersen was one of the thousands of Minnesota Pedersens or Petersens or Petersons. Born and raised in Rochester, Minnesota, where her father was a Professor of Surgery at the Mayo Clinic, she had lived a typical, good, Midwestern, Lutheran life. Tall, blond, blue-eyed—handsome more than pretty—she had a sensual figure in spite of a masculine quality imparted by broad shoulders and somewhat too narrow hips.

In retrospect, her life through high school now struck her as pink, thin and unpalpable—as though she had read about it in a simplistic children's book; as though it were separated from the her that was born again at Radcliffe. Her mother, of course, had opposed the idea of Radcliffe, wanting her to go to Wellesley, where she had gone. She believed in "real" women's schools. They were gentler, somehow more refined, and certainly the quality of education at Wellesley could not be faulted. Sarah, nonetheless, in her first act of direct opposition to her mother (but buttressed by her father's support), elected Radcliffe.

Originally, she had no particular career ambitions, assuming that college was a way station on the road to marriage and children. Almost to her surprise she discovered a fascination with mathematics and economics. She was bright enough to realize that she had no genuine talent for pure mathematics and began to conceive of a role for herself in a world of money and business. With a magna from Radcliffe she dared apply to the Harvard Business School, where she was rejected; she was ten years too early. She came to New York determined to go "where the money was" anyway. She became involved with Jim Burton, a young man who had started his own hedge fund and who was a millionaire five times over by the time he was twenty-eight. It was all so easy in those days. She found she had a knack for security analysis, went to work for him and continued the association even after their sexual relationship had broken off. By the time she was twenty-five she had made a reputation for herself in the Street, and at twenty-eight was invited in as a partner with Burton and Dick Foley. For the past five years the three of them had not had a down year, and had managed a compounded annual growth rate of close to 22 per cent. On the basis of that success they had just started an arbitrage fund. She already had a net worth of close to two million dollars and was one of the half dozen most successful women on Wall Street.

What then, she wondered, is a bright woman like myself doing, living in the middle of an opera? Adam and her life with him could not have been predicted. It should not have happened. If she had read the script she would have rejected it. He had simply showed up one day, like a lost child, at the offices of the volunteers for Bob Kling, during his first campaign for mayor. He seemed confused, bewildered, beautiful and brilliant, all at the same time. He started working as a volunteer at the most tedious and menial level, but his extraordinary analytic abilities almost immediately became apparent. He had mentioned neither his mathematical genius nor his position at Columbia until the fourth or fifth time at the office. By then he had become a fixture and the two of them, a team. After the endorsement of the Democratic Coalition, Kling's shoestring operation caught fire, and for the first time it began to become apparent that Kling had a serious chance for the mayoralty job. The campaign was propelled into an almost hysterical level of work. Adam and she were then thrown together for days on end. He began to confide in her. He told her about his family and his early life. He had never had an intimate, as distinguished from an intellectual, conversation with a woman. It was the beginning of that trust which is the prelude to loving. He was unaware of the fact that she was having an affair with Kling at the time, although it would have been obvious to anyone with any degree of sophistication. She realized that in sexual terms he was totally naïve. She wasn't sure when it was that she first became aware that, despite his age and extraordinary good looks, and in contradiction to the temper of the times, he was almost assuredly still a virgin.

With that recognition, their relationship began to change. His sexual attraction to her broke through his defenses within weeks, and as his struggles with his sexual feelings toward her became more and more obvious, they began to intrude on the easygoing, brother-to-sister type of relationship they had assumed. His unstated anguish, the pathetic yearnings, began to make her feel guilty. She had an enormous capacity for guilt. My God, why am I feeling guilty? she wondered. What have I done?

She began to feel this peculiar responsibility to his sexuality—some urgency to ease his pain. She originally assumed it to be some distorted manifestation of a maternal instinct—a service, an offering to his youth and his innocence. And the more she thought of it that way, the more sexually aroused she became. Eventually it became as much an idée fixe with her as it was with him, but she intuitively knew she would have to wait for his move. She was unaware of how terribly constricted he was, and how slowly he would move forward.

Eventually her frustration became as great as his, and she found herself responding to this unrequited love with the anguish of a pubescent. She did everything to encourage him—yet he seemed paralyzed, insensitive to all her overtures. She had no doubt that he desired her as much as she had come to desire him, but he seemed incapable of recognizing her readiness, her desires for sexual contact.

She had, of course, no aspirations to a full-time relationship. It was to be *Tea and Sympathy* all the way—and then she could retire with the knowledge of a deed well done, and the excitement of having brought a boy to manhood. There would be no emotional attachments, of course, and after a respectable interval of time he would be free to take the gift of potency which she offered to him, and present it to a more suitable partner.

It had all been figured out in her mind if not articulated. Yet he stubbornly resisted making the first move. A smile crossed her face as she thought of some of the grotesquely obvious positions she had put herself in. How many times had she allowed him to catch her in the tub, out of the shower, lying "asleep" under a simple sheet, draped to make a maximum exposure? And then, one day when they were on their way back from Albany, one winter day on an errand for Bob Kling, they were caught in one of those freakish snowstorms, that forced a retreat to a motel, where they registered in the one room available. When he still seemed terrified to announce his desires, she realized she would have to risk approaching him directly; and she did. She pretended she was unaware of his desire for her and cast it in terms of her own needs and passion, which by this point had become not only true, but urgent.

"I want you to sleep with me," she said honestly. "Please don't refuse me. You'll make me feel old and unattractive."

She then undressed in front of him and pulled him down on the bed. He embraced her awkwardly. He was fully clothed still, and hurt her with an intense and frantic crush of kisses and groping. He quickly pulled off his pants and undershorts, as she tried desperately to slow the now almost violent advances. She eased out from under him and guided him over on his back. His penis was erect, its tip moist with preseminal emission. He noticed with embarrassment her looking and instinctively pulled the sheet up over his naked loins. She gently slipped off the Shetland sweater he was wearing, unbuttoned and removed his shirt.

With ignorance and ardor he immediately rolled over and again attempted to penetrate her and to his dismay lost his erection.

"My God, My God," he started to say.

She quickly put her hand across his mouth, and then said softly, "Lie back. Close your eyes. You're too much in a hurry. We have all night."

And she began to make love to him.

On the third attempt he penetrated and had a premature ejaculation. She told him it was wonderful, and he fell asleep in her arms. Only afterwards did she notice that he had not removed his sneakers and sweat socks during the entire period of lovemaking.

A few hours later she began to fondle him as he lay asleep and he became erect. She straddled her half-asleep lover and gently guided his penis into her vagina. Leaning over his body, she kissed him awake. Slowly and gently in a dreamlike state they made love, wonderful love. And he never had a sexual problem with her again. He became the gentle and passionate lover she had rarely encountered in a macho age where so many men equated sex with domination. She was to be not only his first sexual partner, but fatefully, his only one.

When she originally conceived their sexual affair as an "act of service" she had assumed he would find a girl his own age and would shortly leave her. Then she began to dread his finding a younger girl and leaving her. And now he *was* leaving her—but not for another girl. And she was not sure she could bear a life without him; she had never given birth, never raised an infant, and yet she was suffering the most anguishing of human experiences—the premature death of one's child.

Tears started to come, and she fought them back. She shook her head, wiped the back of her hand across her eyes, and rejoined Adam in the bedroom. He had put the books down and his eyes were closed. The last two weeks there had been blessedly no talk of suicide, and she felt mildly reassured. Yet she knew he was preoccupied. He had a way of running his mind in and around a problem, like a piece of automatic machinery, while his consciousness engaged with those about him in seemingly normal conversation. She, however, always knew when she was getting only the edge of his "self" rather than the total involvement which normally characterized their relationship.

She lay on the bed beside him, gently stroking his hair; the radiation and chemotherapy had caused a gradual thinning and he had stopped going to the barber altogether. It was now almost as long as hers. As often happens with chronic illness, his eyes seemed larger, his features more delicate, while she in her blue jeans, wearing his old shirt draped across her broad shoulders could easily have been a boy. Stretched out on the side of the bed she was aware of how much like brother and sister they looked. She smiled to herself, thinking at this point she could easily seem the brother and he the sister.

The touching of his skin aroused her, and she felt an incredible wave of passion. How long had it been since they had made love? Two months? Three months? She wanted him badly, but she didn't care if she only had him this way. In her mind they made love constantly and the fragments of her relationship with him were more than any full relationship she had had before.

She had been talking to him. What on earth had she been saying? she wondered. My God, I'm doing the same thing he does, she thought. We mustn't allow this to separate us. We mustn't discard even the last residue of what we have. He had asked her a question. What was it?

"Did you say kamikaze?" she asked.

"Yes, you know, kamikazes. The ultimate Japanese weapon in World War II."

"The 'ultimate' weapon. Isn't that a little extravagant?" she said with a smile. Why, she thought, must every conversation be about death?

"Not really," he answered. "There's no real defense against it. To the Americans it was inconceivable. It's not our style. We can tolerate death only with uncertainty. We accept a risk, pay for risks, ask people to risk dying in order to construct skyscrapers or bridges—did you know that there is a predictive death rate that is calculated into such jobs?"

"No, I didn't."

"Well, there is," he continued. "Yet we are not a country which would send someone on a suicide mission. Makes you question how 'true' the true believers are in our society. If death is a liberation from the body and the ultimate fusion with Jesus, why in Christ's name don't we all embrace it?

"The Japanese evidently can—or could."

"Oh, yes?"

"And because of that one man, in a small plane, like a human torpedo, could sink a destroyer; and we were defenseless, aghast, bewildered.

"I know you don't like me to talk about these things, but I have to. I only see Moss three times a week, and I've got to talk to someone in between. I don't want to hurt you, and I want you to know I've decided I am not going to kill myself with pills, or stick my head in an oven, or jump off a bridge. I don't want you to be frightened about that."

There was a long pause and then he continued.

"On the other hand, I am not going to lie here while my body rots with cancer and my mind rots with drugs. I've got to have some meaning to my end—if only a negative meaning. I'm going to be a kamikaze."

"Oh, for God's sake, Adam, the war is over. All the wars are over. There are no more kamikazes."

"That's the problem. I have to find a purpose. I have to find my war."

"Adam. You're dying. Don't die as an adolescent!

Forget the romantic nonsense; the world is too large. The issues too diffused. There are no destroyers to sink. There are only buildings to be blown up, by adolescent romantics who injure the innocent in a cause with no goals and a gesture with no purpose. We do not live in an age of grand design. Stop looking for your goddamn dragon."

"You don't think that gestures work? If the assassination against Hitler had been successful..."

"Adam," she interrupted. "There *are* no more Hitlers. We live in a time of large problems and small people. Only whimpers, not bangs."

"Are you aware," he said, obviously not having listened to what she was saying, "how few people it takes to cripple a civilized country? All that is necessary is that the few truly not care whether they live or die. How many terrorists do you think there are in Italy? There can't be more than a hundred and of that hundred—knowing the Italian temperament—less than ten per cent really are prepared to die. A hundred people prepared to die can destroy a Western democracy. Already in northern Italy, as in Western Germany, the wealthy industrialists and political figures are captives of their security systems."

"Adam," she shouted, "Adam, dear God, Adam, listen to me. You are not one of those. You are a brilliant man, but in a different way. You are not an organizer, you are an analyzer. You are not a revolutionary. You are not even to my knowledge a political person. What are you going to do? Bomb the Pentagon? Destroy a nuclear reactor?"

He laughed. "I wasn't thinking of destroying any nuclear devices. If you must know, I was considering building one."

"Jesus Christ! You couldn't!"

"Don't be silly, Sarah. Two slightly better than average college undergraduates have already written theses demonstrating their capacity to construct an atom bomb. I knew more about physics and mathematical technology when I was thirteen than either of the two of them. Constructing the bomb would be no problem for me. But in one sense I'm afraid you're right—I haven't yet the vaguest idea of what practical use I could put it to."

"That's a relief," she interjected.

"Not yet, I said. Not yet. And that's the real problem. You don't think I spend all my hours here simply analyzing methods of destruction. That's the easy part. I'm too good an analyst. I've catalogued a hundred ways of creating havoc that could be effectively performed by one crippled man. But I'm not a destructive person. And I'm not, I don't think, a mean person. I want something to serve—some cause to celebrate—some ideal to sacrifice for. I want to be a kamikaze. So don't worry, dear Sarah, my thoughts are not technical—they're religious!" he said smiling, knowing that it would offend her.

"I'm looking for 'Meaning in Life through a Purposeful Death.'"

Chapter IV

March—sixteen months before the convention

> The East West Cultural Alliance announced appointment to their Board of former President Roger Hilton. Mr. Hilton could not be reached for comment but his close associate James Doyle indicated that it was consistent with Mr. Hilton's long interest in Mideastern affairs and allowed that it would be a reasonable interpretation to assume that this marked his return to a more active creative life. Mr. Doyle strongly emphasized that Mr. Hilton's concerns were cultural and not political.
> (*Time*)

The Knickerbocker Club seemed the ideal location for the meeting. It was discreet, and convenient, being within minutes of the East Side heliport, where Lowell Stoneham maintained a helicopter which would carry Senator Wentworth and himself to their respective jets—waiting at LaGuardia airport. Both men were in town attending a Board of Directors' meeting of Interbank. With Kate Parr, of course, there was no problem. Midtown Manhattan was her home territory. Admiral Mudd had decided it would be unnecessary for him to attend as long as Hugh Baker would be present. For Baker it was important to keep trips to New York to a minimum. His anonymity was a crucial part of his functioning and Washington was a natural habitat in which his presence was unremarkable. He was a Washington bureaucrat among Washington bureaucrats. This occasion was of such importance that it warranted the risk.

Stoneham and Wentworth had been lunching together in a private room when they were discreetly joined by the other two. Stoneham, automatically acting as host, had ordered a glass of sherry for Kate Parr, and a glass of white wine for Hugh Baker.

Small talk continued for some ten minutes—enough to add a note of civility. During that period Lowell Stoneham observed Hugh Baker toying with the glass of wine. It was his traditional drink and yet he almost invariably left the glass untouched. He rarely took a sip from it. Stoneham suspected that Baker was a closet teetotaler. Stoneham, himself, enjoyed liquor, as he enjoyed all sensual things, and he tended to distrust ascetics. Somehow or other, despite all the control, the formalism and the steeliness of the exterior man, Baker simply did not fit into the stereotype of a monastic. This was not an inert stone, but a coiled, powerful spring; the housing had to be rigid to contain the latent power. Stoneham wondered, and a small smile began to glide across his face. Of course! Not a teetotaler, not at all. Quite the contrary, an alcoholic. A reformed alcoholic! Those were the other nondrinkers of the world. He liked the idea and was pleased with himself for having analyzed the problem and arrived at what—

with absolute self-confidence—he assumed was the correct answer. Stoneham now liked Baker more than before. Damn it, he thought, I really don't know much about that man.

He noticed Kate Parr looking at him quizzically, perhaps observing his smile. There was a passionate woman, Stoneham knew without a fragmentary doubt. A lifetime womanizer, he had never lost his interest in beautiful women, or his capacity to appreciate them. Lucky McAllister, he thought. Her devotion was apparent to the world, but what intrigued Stoneham the most was his speculation about their private hours. He had an eye for beauty, whether male or female, and his mind constructed quick, flashing scenarios of the beautiful nude bodies of Lincoln McAllister and Kate Parr linked in various exotic, and erotic, embraces. He imagined himself now with Kate Parr—she would have those long sinuous legs of California beach girls, and he imagined them wrapped around his body, her foot sliding softly against his leg and up his thigh. He began to feel a fullness in his groin and was delighted at his continuing capacity for quick erections, even with simple fantasy at an age when most men had difficulty in fact. He wondered if Kate Parr were available for a dalliance. He suspected not. Too involved, too totally involved with Lincoln McAllister. No, he could not conceive of moving into that territory—at least not for the present. And the future, well, the future could always bring almost anything. Stoneham, despite his singular frustrations in pursuit of the presidency, remained an optimist. His reverie was interrupted by John Wentworth's voice gradually breaking the surface of consciousness.

"You had said, Mr. Baker, that there was a matter of some urgency, I believe."

"Yes, Senator," Baker replied. "And perhaps it *is* time to get down to the reason for the meeting. Both the Admiral and I respect the latitude and autonomy you've granted us in this operation. It has allowed for that freedom that alone safeguards security; it insures that our plan will evolve according to its own timetable rather than to an imposed one, determined by accident or a smart newspaperman. However, at this point the Admiral feels the need for some specific advice."

"The Admiral has never needed our advice, or consent," Stoneham observed wryly. "He knows we're all intimidated by him."

"Oh, come now, Lowell," Wentworth interrupted.

"You don't like the word intimidated, Jack?" Lowell continued. "All right, call it what you want—respect, awe, admiration. It's all the same shit. The Admiral damn well knows he doesn't need our advice and consent, even if you don't. The fact that he occasionally asks for it is a testament not just to his courtesy, but to his damn good sense. But when he asks for it—hold on to your wallets, boys—the ante is going up. We understand meetings like this aren't held as celebration; so get on with the bad news, my boy."

"Well, there is reason for some celebration," Baker continued. "We have had enormous co-operation from the press; the corporate world has come around; we are making progress in the academic community; and it goes without saying that the philanthropic institutions are falling all over themselves to get into line. We are, however, having our problems with Congress. With elections coming up they are balking and although some of Hilton's old stalwarts are co-operating with a vengeance—we don't really need or want that. The most important need is passivity. We must have a mass that remains neutral. Support isn't necessary. We cannot afford any organized opposition from within our own party, or from the Democrats. The whole idea of this is to bury The Scandal. We must not have newspaper headlines of the wrong kind. Some Congressmen, despite the Admiral's personal intervention, seem unable to comprehend the importance we attach to Red Herring. They are going to need some more effective convincing. We are going to have to play it a little rougher."

"You suggested that at the last meeting, Hugh. I think Steve Cross asked you precisely what that meant and you sashayed around the question. Now, what is it you want to do?"

"Well," Baker continued, "you and Jack know about

the Pandora Files. Miss Parr, perhaps it is time you know. Over the years we have collected a set of private files gleaned from various sources on all the major figures in the government. These files are primarily research tools to help in the selection of future candidates; in the prediction of Senate and House voting; and in the trustworthiness of individuals. Of course they contain much that is personal, private and devastating."

"But there has been a general understanding that that stuff will *never* be used except for the good of the country and then only via the methods of private persuasion," Wentworth said.

"For over thirty years, there has been a gentleman's agreement that that file was sacrosanct. We all have a certain, shall I say, vulnerability," Lowell Stoneham continued with an edge of anguish in his voice. "And we have all been allowed to sleep in peace with the tacit agreement that the stuff will never be used. Are you now telling me you are prepared to open that fucking Pandora's box? Who's clean enough to take the lid off? Not even the Admiral, I'd wager—or maybe only the Admiral. Are you that cocky, Hugh? It seems to me you may have a few guilty things buried away in the corners."

Baker felt a slight flush but continued, "Under ordinary conditions we wouldn't consider it. But the intransigence must be overcome. It is time that is the enemy. We have to move them. We have to convince them that we mean business and we don't have time for our usual persuasive methods."

"How can you do that?" Kate Parr asked, intrigued at what, to her, was an awareness of a new element in the game.

There was a silence for a moment and then Baker continued, "There are a good many people whose cooperation we require. All we ask of this majority is silence, not for approbation. In order to move the large number we simply have to hurt a few. We need to let that majority know that we are in extremis. The Admiral has proposed to make two small sacrifices to set an example of the seriousness of our purposes."

"My God, they are all our friends," Wentworth protested.

"This is all simply contingency planning at this point," Baker continued. "Nothing is yet definite. And if we must move ahead we will use only our two sacrificial lambs, and they will be offered gently. And then, let me repeat, only if needed. I underline that—only if needed."

"What's the last chapter then? Who, when and what?" Stoneham demanded.

"We thought that we would start with one of our own," Baker said. "Oliphant is retiring from the Senate. His *career* therefore will not be damaged. It will be over already. He is an older man and what we will choose to leak will hurt, but not damage excessively. We are not out to kill anybody."

"But these are our friends," Wentworth repeated, his voice cracking as he licked his drying lips.

"Precisely so, Senator. We must indicate our sense of urgency and priority and we do that by starting at the highest, with one of our own. If that should not work and only if that should not work, we will then move to Jack Watson."

"Oh, no! Not Jack," said Stoneham almost involuntarily. Jack Watson—while a Democrat and from the Boston slums that were as antithetical a background as one could imagine from the Main-Line, St. Paul's tradition of Stoneham—had nonetheless over the years become one of Lowell Stoneham's few friends drawn from his political life. "Why Jack?"

"He is a Democrat and we must let those fellows know they must join us—and he's the power in the House. I hope it will come to neither, but if the crunch comes we will release information on the two of them. The rest will then get the message. We start with our friends because then they know we mean business. If our friends are forced to pay a price, we will have delivered the message with conviction to those about whom we are less concerned. We simply have to have total co-operation for Red Herring to work. I repeat, we will only release enough information to hurt, not destroy. I promise you no one will go to jail."

Kate Parr shuddered to herself upon recalling the conversation as she left the club. She walked from Sixty-second Street down Fifth Avenue simply to get some fresh air and to collect herself. She had been shaken by what had just happened, and it had been a long time since she had found herself shocked. She had known for a long time that she was playing in the big leagues, and presumed that she could tough it out with the best men in the business. But this made her feel frightened and vulnerable. It was not the brutality; it was the coolness. The dedication to purpose that transcended friendship, feelings, sensibility or compassion. All her adult life she had been convinced that there were no essential differences between a strong man and a strong woman. She wondered now. She would go along, of course, but could she initiate such action? It frightened her, and Kate Parr was not used to fear. She had been so shaken up she had not precisely heard what Baker had said to her in private as they were leaving. This was unlike her. She had a memory that rarely failed—in great part because she had focus; she knew how to concentrate her attention. As an English major at Bryn Mawr she had learned that words carried precise meanings—and exact recall was critical. But she had been preoccupied. She wanted desperately to remember the words, so that she neither overvalued nor underestimated the intention. He had referred to Link and then gently but persuasively suggested that the Admiral thought the time was approaching for Link to make some small gesture. Yes, that was it. "Some small gesture." It was all said so casually, but in the context of the meeting she knew that Link would have to move and move quickly. He dare not incur the anger of these men. No, anger was the wrong word, she thought. These men do not indulge in anger. He must not disappoint them. For the first time she had the sense that even Link was simply a small, albeit important, relay point in a complex system. Even he was only a bit player in this vast scenario.

Chapter V

June—thirteen months before the convention

> Former President Roger Hilton was in the receiving stand for the Memorial Day Parade in Columbus, Ohio. He had accepted an honorary degree the previous day from the Union Baptist Seminary. (Columbus *Dispatch*)

Peter Moss was sitting beside his pool in Scarsdale, eating a lunch of chicken sandwiches and iced tea with his wife, Ann. Peter was tired. He had arisen at 7:00 A.M.—angry with himself for not being able to sleep later. He needed the rest; he felt stretched thin; irritable; and unsatisfied with himself. He needed, what? Not rest—respite. R&R—the Navy term came to mind.

He had eased out of bed carefully so as not to disturb Ann, quickly slipped on a tee shirt, chinos and an old pair of sneakers. Peter liked physical work; he liked the concreteness and tangibility; he liked the steady visible signs of progress made; he liked the predictability of the product at the end—all things lacking in his work as a psychoanalyst.

They had bought the old house in Scarsdale for its beautiful setting in an extraordinary garden of giant rhododendrons, azaleas massive with years of careful pruning, and roses—walls and walls of old climbing roses with the thick, gnarled stems that measure age and continuity. The house, itself, had been converted from a nondescript 1920s mongrel—to a bastardized, eclectic, romantic modern that represented not only the Mosses' taste, but their sweat and labor. During the years when their children were growing up he would unwind with saws and lumber, Sheetrock and paint. Cursing at unplumbed walls and bad miters—and draining all his real tensions in the mock frustration of the physical labor he loved.

But now, after all these years, there was not even busy work that he could find in the house. They had made an environment that was theirs and they were happy with it. But the garden was different. Thank God for the garden. A constantly changing battle for, with and against nature. He had spent himself, literally, in the garden, working until his middle-aged muscles ached, and his hands were cut and sore (he hated garden gloves—they were a barrier between himself and the earth) to a point he could not ignore, and now he was ready to relax. Sprawled on the chaise longue, he was trying to catch his wife's conversation as his mind perversely and independently sought passages and entries into areas he was struggling to avoid.

"I feel sorry for Elizabeth Hilton," Ann continued. "It was bad enough having to share a life with Hilton; then to go through The Scandal and the disgrace; then the isolation; and now the mastectomy. I gather from the reports that there is really not much hope for her."

"Uh-hum," said Moss, not really listening.

"There's a picture of her leaving the hospital in this week's *Newsweek*. Why is it that she seems so vulnerable? Why is it that certain people seem destined to be victims and others victimizers? There is a quality, even in that photo, that makes you distrust and dislike Roger Hilton, in the same way that his wife always appears a pathetic and vulnerable creature."

"Yes."

"Yes?" she laughed. "What does 'yes' mean? You haven't heard a word I said. What are you thinking about?"

"Nothing," he said.

"Nothing means that boy. You're thinking about Adam again."

Peter looked embarrassed. For years he had shielded his wife and children from the problems of his practice. The privacy of the patient was a basic tenet he valued highly. Inevitably, his family began to identify some of his more public patients—his daughters would snicker when he'd turn on a television program for which he would normally have no essential interest. But while absolute privacy was impossible, it remained a central principle. His wife never questioned the opening nights or the art openings which he loathed, but which inevitably indicated some patient's involvement. Yet a kind of dignified game was played; even when his wife was sure of the names of his patients—and, after all, she did deposit his checks—she avoided direct or explicit acknowledgment. But Adam was different. In every way that damned boy was different. For one thing, unlike most patients, Adam called the house, left his name, and even talked, in an absentminded way, with Ann Moss when Peter was out of town.

All of the rules seemed to have been broken for him—or by him. It was not that Peter had not suffered with other patients. Professional distancing is always an imperfect shield for the professional, so he suffered with all of his patients. But the boy was different; his youth, his brilliance, his potential, his vulnerability, his insistence on blatantly treating Peter as though he were a father rather than a physician. Finally, the anguish of sharing the sheer physical pain and the hopelessness of Adam's life made Peter feel that his paternalistic feelings might be the only thing he had to offer.

"Yes," Moss continued. "At least indirectly. It is Adam again. I'm thinking of going to the APA meetings this Christmas."

"You, going to the APA meetings? Twenty years as a psychiatrist and you've never attended one psychiatric convention."

"Maybe it has been a mistake. There are certain things one doesn't get from articles and I suddenly realize how few friends I have in the profession; I mean friend-friends—the kind you talk with and end up feeling reassured. Of course it is the boy. He is getting to me, and I need someone to talk to about him. I should have gone to the meetings in the spring. There was a panel on treatment of the dying patient."

"You could always talk to me—I always thought of

myself as your friend," she said, half hurt, half bantering.

Peter recognized the foolishness of his reserve. It was built into his life like the crossbeams and support structures of a house. Home was home; office was office; and never the twain ought meet. To talk about Adam to a friend, like Skip, was to talk about a theoretical case, to talk with a colleague was discussing a patient. With Ann he would be talking about his patient to his wife—he would be violating a confidence; but what confidence? Adam Haas had already exposed himself to Ann. My God, he not only talked to her, he teased her! She was used to an occasional call from other patients, and invariably it involved a constrained, hesitant voice asking "if the doctor was home"; and half the time—before the words were completely out—the terrified and unidentified patient would hang up. With Adam by the very second call it had been: "Hello, Ann, this is Adam, again. How are you?" The first names unsettled her; and the direct address threw her completely. She sputtered "fine" like a flustered schoolgirl and fled to find Peter. He called with a certain degree of regularity, if not frequently, and always with the insouciance of a close member of the family—not the reserve expected of a patient. When Peter was not available he would leave complicated messages whose intimacy and candor at first appalled her and later beguiled her. She felt she knew Adam, and worse, was beginning to grow fond of him.

Peter recognized the stupidity of pretending any more, and with an enormous sense of relief began talking about his problems with Adam. Ironically, it was not Adam he was exposing, but himself. It was his anguish, pain, doubts and frustrations.

He talked about the steady decline in Adam's strength, the deterioration of his body and the peculiarly morbid method he was utilizing to come to grips with his impending death.

"But something is changing," Peter said. "I didn't mind the violent fantasies; it seemed to me they served a purpose. But now I don't know; the lines between fantasy and reality are getting blurred—but not in the usual direction. It's not that he's confusing his fantasies with reality—that would be slipping into psychotic thinking—and that I understand. This seems to be the opposite—it's as though he is working to force reality to conform to his fantasies and it..."

"I'm not sure I follow," Ann said. "What do you mean?"

"Well," he sighed, "his dreams are always filled with violence, but that's nothing new; they have always been. What has changed, what worries me now, is the specificity of the details. There's information in the dreams of an expertise that he never had. It means he's studying. He's absolutely brilliant, you know, and ingenious. He's got a mathematician's mind and the hands of a fine toolmaker. These are not just his usual primary process dreams about his own death or his impotence; they deal with the technical aspect of armaments. He now knows about rifle bores, machine guns, television sights, bombs, explosives. The information comes up in his associations and the details of his dreams. It may mean nothing.

"But it isn't just in his dreams. More and more, in his waking associations, he's talking about wanting his death to have some purpose. He's fascinated by the Red terrorists, and while he has contempt for their political anarchy, he envies them a cause to die for. I have a feeling I'm dealing with a human torpedo ready for launching and simply waiting for a target."

"What target?" asked Ann. "The Vietnam War is over. Blowing up the Pentagon would serve no purpose. There's nothing to protest except the stupidity and banality and vulgarity of modern life. And then what do you do? Blow up Regine's? Or the offices of *People* magazine?"

"I don't know. And that may be what saves him. He's talking of stopping his chemotherapy, you know. And if he does, he'll be dead, or a vegetable in less than two months. I don't think it will be the latter. I know him; he'll kill himself before he allows that. He's as much as told me, and that doesn't bother me. In a sense I've been an accomplice. I've not restricted his access to pain-killing drugs and he could accumulate enough in a month to end it all. I would do the same, I suspect. At least, I would want to do the same.

"It's an act of social violence that frightens me. Fortunately he's not a terribly political person and he's a completely rational one. Besides, he's getting progressively more helpless. He would never do something harmful or destructive to the innocent. There is an essential gentleness to the boy. He'd have to have a target and for him, at least, a good reason."

"There are no good reasons for terrorism," she said.

"For you and me there may not be. For him there may be. And I am concerned. I am sure it's irrelevant, but if he should concoct some scheme, what am I to do with it? Even if I were reasonably positive he would not act—would I be remiss in not reporting it? My God, I'd be right in the middle of a double agent problem."

"What in the world is a double agent problem?" she asked.

"It all started with the Russian psychiatry mess. Then American psychiatry began to suspect that we should start looking into our own household affairs. If a psychiatrist works for an airline and a pilot comes to him for consultation, whose agent is the psychiatrist? Who is he serving, the company or the patient? You know the whole of psychiatry is built on the trust of the patient that the psychiatrist is serving his purposes alone. Christ, I have had a dozen patients confiding in me breaches in morality, and even law. It is not my responsibility to call the IRS about a patient I am treating who's cheating on his taxes. It would be the utmost in irresponsibility. I have even had patients who have committed felonies, and, again, I have assumed that was for the police to resolve, not for me. But I've never had one *about* to commit a crime!

"With the adolescent it's a real agony. Whose agent am I? Theirs or their parents? When a young adolescent is playing around with drugs and I know about it, is my responsibility to their privacy or to their future? Are they independent moral agents of their own or should I be sharing this information with their parents?"

"Are you thinking of Adam's parents and his potential suicide?"

"No, I think I have resolved that. There my primary responsibility is to his privacy and his trust in treatment. Oh, Christ, I don't know. Maybe I'm only saying that in his case suicide seems rational, while other things don't. I only worry if his violent death might include others—then what would I do?"

"Peter, what do you mean, what would you do? Of course you would prevent it."

"Ann, I've never been faced with it. How the hell do I know what I'd do? I don't have those kind of patients or those kinds of problems. It isn't quite so easy as an 'of course.' It would be an agony for me to betray that boy."

"To save an innocent life? To save a decent and unwitting bystander?" she asked incredulously.

"Oh, shit, the whole thing is stupid, theoretical and totally irrelevant. My God, he's a vegetarian on principles. I can't imagine his swatting a fly. He would never take an innocent life. He would never destroy a decent person."

"Then I don't understand what your dilemma is. I really don't follow you. I don't know what you are saying."

"Maybe I don't either. Maybe it's a tempest in a teapot. Maybe I need a vacation."

Chapter VI

June—thirteen months before the convention

Hand-delivered confidential letter to Horace Mudd from Hugh Baker

Dear Admiral:

Things are going well, much better than I had anticipated. I am confident that once the momentum is reached, Operation Red Herring will have been able to achieve its major goal. Stephen Cross has indicated to me his "dissatisfaction with the pace" of the operation. He feels that our "slant" is wrong; that it is not sufficient to simply make Hilton less a villain, i.e., no longer an object of hatred, but rather we must create an object of public guilt. "We must make him a martyr." I explained to Cross that we cannot plan on making him an heroic figure in three years. If we can make him an object of pity, we can build from there. I promised him "eventual martyrdom."

Speaking of martyrs—what about poor Elizabeth? It is horrible to think this way, but Elizabeth's breast cancer was a fortuitous event. I have arranged to have an honorary degree from Southern Christian Seminary in Mississippi conferred on Hilton. It was not hard. For next spring I have at least three honorary degrees lined up, none of them wanted to be the first—so the principle of momentum once again proves its importance. I am finally breaking away from seminaries and small right-wing colleges.

I'm sorry that the exposure of the Oliphant involvement in the Korean scandals caused such an immediate stir. I'm afraid we underestimated how sensitive that issue still is. I know that the Senator is an old friend of yours and I had thought that the little bit we had made public was trivial enough to protect his public image. I have assurances from Jimmy Saperstein that the people in the press will drop it shortly. It has had its desired effect in the Senate. I think that the Watson release about the Bolivian tin deal now scheduled for leakage in three weeks—we thought this less volatile than his Chilean involvements—will get the message to the House and the Democrats. The state party chairmen are already beginning to come around and at least in the South and the Rocky Mountain States he will be guaranteed some speaking engagements.

The press coverage has been beyond our expectations. (You might, if you have time, sir, drop Jimmy a letter congratulating him. He would greatly appreciate it.) And the Good Lord seems to be on our side. His becoming a grandfather is going to be an enormous help. Now, if only they were triplets!

Respectfully,
HUGH B.

P.S. I just received a call from Senator Wentworth's office. He is always so careful on the telephone that I am never exactly sure I understand what he is saying. But I think he has promised to name Hilton to the Board of the Wentworth Foundation, any time after January 1, of election year. I had tried to press him for an earlier appointment but he feels he is in too public a position. He has promised to arrange some corporate directorships during the course of next year. I generally have not burdened you with specific details of the operation, but I thought you would be pleased to know that Wentworth is truly co-operating.

Chapter VII

July—twelve months before the convention

> Ex-President and Mrs. Roger Hilton were guests at a large party at the Southampton estate of Stephen Cross. The party was attended by a number of politically influential people...(New York *Daily News*)

She had the cabdriver stop at the corner of Sixty-third and Park Avenue, paid him hurriedly and ran the quarter block to Quo Vadis. She was only a few minutes late, but Kate Parr prided herself on her punctuality and was annoyed at the traffic jam that had detained her for fifteen minutes. The doorman opened the door, and she quickly entered one of the few quiet restaurants still left in New York City. Vito nodded his recognition as he efficiently ushered her to the banquette in the rear where Lincoln McAllister and his wife, Alison, were already sitting.

Alison McAllister had been born to a comfortable, but not affluent branch of the New England Coolidges—a family as distinguished for its intellectual achievements as its philanthropies. Her father, a small-town newspaper publisher in the Northeast Kingdom of Vermont had assumed—long before it was fashionable—that a woman required as rigorous an education as a man. She had gone to Milton Academy and then had elected Swarthmore College over Radcliffe—in the first serious act of overt defiance of parental authority, indicating the independence her father had, theoretically at least, hoped for in his daughter! Her chagrined—and doting—father had of course acquiesced. While at Milton, she had been best friends with "Buffy" McAllister, Lincoln's younger sister. The seeds of the romance that was to blossom into love were thus set at sixteen.

Charles Coolidge had hoped for a political career for his daughter, and was not at all pleased with Alison's decision to marry at twenty-one—even to a distinguished young McAllister. He was, needless to say, now totally delighted with his son-in-law—particularly acknowledging his respect, even dependence, on Alison's judgments and values.

No man has a right to have as much as Lincoln McAllister—wealth, an incredibly successful business career and early political success. Blessed by nature with a body that seemed designed by Praxiteles, and endowed with an athlete's reflexes, he had become an Olympic light heavyweight wrestler, the only American ever to win a silver medal. Given all this, the public could never acknowledge that such a man could not be a playboy. The fact that he was a constant man, as fastidious in his moral life as in his dress, would be an affront to the fantasies of the nation, and could not be accepted. Kate, herself, had at first been offended that he had never made a pass at her. While she had had a woman as a lover for some five years, she did enjoy the sexual companionship of men on occasion and felt rejected by the passes that were not made. Only with time was she aware that his moral rectitude, and a rather low threshold of sexuality precluded the promiscuity which the general public inevitably assumed. Perhaps, she mused, this was why he was capable of accepting women as people and as equals in a way that few men were. He took their opinions seriously and he never patronized.

Kate noticed that Link had already ordered a bottle of white wine, which he had placed on the table as he rose to greet her. Instead of his traditional Pouilly-Fuissé, he had expansively indulged in a bottle of Montrachet, and she recognized with a sense of guilt and regret that she was intruding on what had been intended as a tête-à-tête.

The relationship was close enough so that little time was wasted on the social amenities, the pleasantries and the apology for lateness. Then Kate started in.

"Alison, I'm sorry to have co-opted what I understand had originally been planned as a private lunch. I know how few you have these days. I simply had to talk to Lincoln. I just got off the phone with Hugh Baker and he is worried."

"About what?" interrupted McAllister.

"About Red Herring," she replied.

"About Red Herring!" he sneered. "My God, I should have thought he was having a celebration. You can't pick up a paper or magazine any more without seeing that name intruded in the public consciousness."

"Link," Alison said reprovingly, disturbed by the aggressive and acerbic quality of his response to Kate. "Link, you should be pleased. This is being done for you. For your election. The only thing that stands between you and the presidency is the image of that man.

The party must remove it. What difference does it make if a defeated old man is seen as victim rather than victimizer? Your hostility to him has spilled over into the whole project. I don't understand you. You've always been a practical man."

"He's an evil person," Link responded. "And he deserves the kind of social disgrace, ostracism and humiliation that has been meted out to him. He deserves more!"

"For God's sake, Link, we don't live in an age of perfect justice," Alison responded. "You're no adolescent. You know the men in white hats do not always win. Yet with Roger Hilton you persist in this intemperate rage."

"Alison, I shouldn't have to remind you of all people, but I barely got out of that mess with my integrity and my career intact."

"But you did get out," she responded. "Because you *did* have the integrity, and no one now associates you with Hilton. We're talking merely of revamping his image."

"Now they have you talking like a PR man—'revamping his image'—as though there is no truth, there is no essential quality to a person, only images. My God, we're all beginning to sound like Jimmy Saperstein."

"I apologize for the term," Alison said. "And you are right. The man deserves more than what he got. We, more than most, know that. But all we are talking about is allowing the man to return to a normal and undeservedly respected social life. Am I right, Kate?" she asked, turning to the woman who had been silently taking this all in. "We are not planning a role for him in the government. He will never ever again have any power to guide the destiny of this country or to destroy its institutions. You will see to that, Link. You keep forgetting, you will be at the seat of power. You will be in command. You will be able to veto any suggestions, if they arise, that Red Herring go beyond a social rehabilitation. What is it that concerns you? Why are you anxious?"

"I'm not anxious," he answered with an edge of anger, again so atypical of him that it alerted both women.

"Is there something that we both don't know, Link?" Kate asked. Catching a sharp look in his eye, and not wanting to antagonize him further, she softened the question. "Is there some aspect of this you see, some danger you anticipate, that we haven't analyzed well enough? Some calculation we should be considering? Alison is right. No one, to my knowledge, is planning any active role for him in the political process."

"He'll want it. You know damn well he'll want it," Link answered.

"What he wants is unimportant," Kate continued. "What we are doing now—the entire Red Herring operation—has nothing to do with what *he* wants. It's what *we* want, and what we want, Link, is to see you in the presidency."

There was a pause, as though the awesomeness of the goal that seemed now within reach had sobered all three of them.

The headwaiter, almost as if sensing the need for an interlude, beckoned the waiter to serve the light lunch McAllister had ordered for all of them. The eel with green sauce was carefully served with a salad of arugala and Belgian endive, and the waiter retired.

After a moment Link spoke. "If only I were sure. Sure that that man could be contained."

"What can he do, Link?" Kate asked. "He has no power. He has no following. There is only poor Jim Doyle, who stuck it out with him. That's hardly an army."

"Maybe it isn't. And maybe it is." And then he continued after a pause, "There is always Horace Mudd."

"Link," exclaimed Alison with shock in her voice. "You don't distrust Admiral Mudd!"

"At this point I don't know whom I trust and whom I don't. Who is working for whom. I don't like the game plan. No one is quite what he seems. We live in a world of 'images,' as you just reminded me. I only know that Horace has immense power which, I grant, he has never chosen to exercise for venal purposes—at least to my knowledge—and never for his own aggrandizement.

But he has the power, and I now see him manipulating the entire country, and I don't like it."

Link seemed to be talking to himself with a loquacity unusual for him. Alison flashed a concerned quizzical look to Kate, whose almost imperceptible shrug expressed her ignorance of why Link seemed so distraught.

"I hear Baker's voice behind every commentator," Link continued, "behind every column. I see his hand in every society page, at every board meeting, at every philanthropic organization. I cannot tell you the number of meetings now in which the words, those obscene words, Roger Hilton, are now raised. Words that weren't uttered in decent society for two years except as an oath or an expletive. His name just 'comes up.'"

Something is wrong, Kate realized. Something's very wrong. Link is holding something back—and not just from me—from Alison. She was frightened.

"People wonder what he is doing," Link went on. "People comment on his wife or her sickness. His granddaughter. It all seems by chance and yet they have all been handled by unseen agents and they are not aware for whom the agents work. I am simply not sure what private plans Horace Mudd and Hugh Baker have for *me*."

Chapter VIII

July—twelve months before the convention

> Roger Hilton was an unexpected addition to the list of attendants at the upcoming conference on "Society and Public Policy" sponsored by UNESCO to be held in Paris in September. (Washington *Post*)

Stephen Cross sat at an enormous rosewood desk, fingering, unopened, a letter handed to him by his secretary. It was in a simple, unmarked, long business envelope with a discreet injunction typed in the left-hand corner: "Personal and Confidential. To be opened by Mr. Cross only."

He knew of course that it was from Roger Hilton. Two weeks earlier he had had lunch with Hilton at the Union Club in Philadelphia. The night before they had both attended the annual dinner of the Alliance Français. The fact that Roger Hilton had even been invited, indicated how rapidly things had moved since launching Operation Red Herring; the fact that he and Hilton had felt free to have lunch together in public showed how self-confident Hilton was beginning to be. Cross was anxious about this; he knew the pent-up rage, the coiled-spring readiness for revenge, that existed in Hilton, and, while ready to serve it, he did not want that tension released too early. Cross had the conservatism of a good corporate lawyer; he knew that waiting won most of the games and that the victory went to the tenacious, not the tempestuous.

If it were recognized prematurely that Cross was not serving Red Herring, but was actually Hilton's agent, it would be destructive to the ultraconservative unit of the party they both served; would hinder their reassertion of authority and power; and would represent a personal disaster for Cross, himself. He was sophisticated enough to know the limits, as well as the measure, of his own power. He knew there was no winning a direct confrontation with the Admiral. As far as Admiral Mudd was concerned it was essential that Cross be regarded as simply another member of the team. Admiral Mudd did not yet suspect Cross of being Hilton's man—of this Cross was certain. If he had, Cross reasoned, he would not be privy to the most intimate planning of Red Herring. To his knowledge Hugh Baker reported directly only to the seven people who had met that day in September aboard the *Five Star Final,* and in addition, to Jim Doyle, Hilton's companion, surrogate and lackey. It was essential that Baker and Mudd succeed in their plan for Cross and Hilton to succeed in their own. He trusted Hilton enough to know that he made no assumptions based on wishful thinking. Hilton had the stick to use when the time was ripe. No, the hard part was not seizing power, the hard part was gaining respectability. That was the only platform from which authority could be seized—and that could only be accomplished by Mudd.

He was worried about Hilton. He was so hungry for power and vengeance that he might not wait. Cross himself would have been happier moving slower—preferring even a semi-public or semi-private luncheon in Philadelphia—but Hilton had pressed, and he had acquiesced. So far things had moved well, almost too well, and Cross was uneasy. He preferred complications. He was used to resolving them. Complications were analyzable, and the small units dissected out were subject to correction and modification.

He looked at the letter once again. Then opened it.

Steve:

I am pleased with the progress of Red Herring. It is moving beyond even my expectations. Would you believe I am beginning now to get direct solicitations for speaking engagements and even for appointments to various boards and commissions. I've accepted none of them directly. I continue to play the game and I first refer all such requests to Baker. God, that is one creepy man! I never even see him as a human being. Just as an extension of Horace Mudd. Does he ever have a thought of his own? Have you ever seen any emotions in him? Or is he just Mudd's robot? At any rate, I've been "a good boy." Eating all their shit, kissing ass for each of their condescending and patronizing "favors."

They are committed, and, as far as I can tell, there is no way back. I've decided, then, it is time for us to move Killer Whale.

I know your conservative bias, but we cannot wait forever. You are not going to like this but I have dispatched Jim to New York. The primary reason is that I have decided to move back to Westchester. I know this is going to disturb "the boys" but I can't operate out of this backwater place anymore. I've got to be closer to where things are happening.

Sooner or later, that smug, tightass McAllister is going to have to give me a public hug. Why haven't they moved him before this? I'm thinking of having Jim drop in on him. Unless that bastard gets moving soon it's going to be apparent to the public that he doesn't accept me. If he doesn't acknowledge me, the rest means nothing. Red Herring will go down the drain.

RH

Damn the man, thought Cross. Why can't he wait? Cross was just as disturbed that McAllister was still playing coy so late in the game, but he knew that Mudd must be equally conscious of the foot dragging—and would eventually do something about it. Mudd knew these power plays better than any of them, and if Hilton and he were aware of it now, Mudd certainly was aware of it at least a month earlier—and was already working on it.

On the other hand, he thought, the move to New York might be a smart one. It would, of course, alert Baker—everything alerted that man! But to what? To the fact that Hilton was impatient, and only that. He had no way of knowing that there was another fish swimming the same waters as Red Herring. Only he, Cross, Hilton, Jim Doyle, and soon—but for God's sake not yet—McAllister would know that.

He quickly grabbed a piece of yellow legal stationery and typed:

Dear R,

The move to Westchester seems fine. But trust me, and *do not*, I beg you, *do not* send Jim on the mission.

STEVE

He folded it, put it in a plain business envelope, addressed it and marked it "Personal and Confidential."

Chapter IX

October—nine months before the convention

> James Doyle acknowledged that former President Roger Hilton had purchased a home in Briarcliff Manor. According to Mr. Doyle, Mr. Hilton planned to move his headquarters to New York shortly to facilitate his increasing attention to philanthropic problems. (New York *Times*)

Adam was lying stretched out on the sling in the bathtub—somewhat at peace. He had taken a Demerol and two Empirins half an hour before. The effects of the drugs had sufficiently eased the pain so that, combined with the flotation in the tepid water, he had achieved a state of blessed relief.

He had recently begun to use crutches in the house, although in the few forays he made alone outside he persisted in trying to make his way with a cane. He had been depressed all afternoon with the recognition that the pain was simply too much, the dangers too great and that soon he would have to begin to use crutches in the street. He had passed, he realized, another landmark. There were very few left.

Sarah had been talking about a wheelchair, at least for within the house, and while he had resisted the idea he recognized it was inevitable. To resist would be an act of selfishness and self-deceit. The wheelchair was as essential for her as it was for him. He had come to use her support in a physical as well as a psychological sense, and only this evening had it occurred to him that the weight of both might be draining even her stamina. She had seemed to grow stronger as he had grown weaker. Tonight she had made a joke that it might be easier if she simply carried him into the bath. She had the strong, broad shoulders of a farm girl and with his weight now down to about 115 pounds he would not have been surprised at all if she could have managed it.

Sarah was in the kitchen finishing off the dinner dishes, chattering away in her usual incessant and cheerful way. She wondered if he really listened these days. But it didn't matter. She knew he enjoyed the flow of talk. As he became quieter she became almost garrulous.

"You can't pick up a magazine these days without seeing McAllister in it. Not that I mind, God, that man is handsome. The party seems to be already solidly behind him. No one else is ever mentioned. Is it possible that this early we already know who our next President is going to be?"

She was walking around barefoot, with nothing on except running shorts and an old sweat shirt of Adam's. She enjoyed the evenings together, when he had just received his medication and was relatively free of pain and they could try, at least for a few moments, to forget his illness. Forget was a funny word since their entire life was molded by his dying. She dressed and undressed him, bathed him, and helped him maneuver his way through the daily chores that had once been mechanical and unexamined, but now represented so much agony. She was his messenger, his servant, his mother, his friend, everything except his lover.

She came into the bathroom, still chattering away, quickly pulled the sweat shirt off in one deft movement, took the newspaper out of his hand, kissed him on the forehead and on both eyes.

"I'm going to give you a bath now," she said.

She kneeled down on a piece of foam rubber she kept by the side of the tub. The bath was a ritual. It relaxed him. He was often at his most peaceful and she loved the physical contact. She used no washcloth, wanting the fine tuning of fingertip touch on his body, carefully recognizing which joints were swollen, which limbs needed special care and movement. She knew his body like her own; no, better. She knew which touches pleased, and where potential pain lay. It was their primary sensual contact and, while not directly sexual, it surely was not free from sexual pleasures for her. She loved the physical touch of her soapy fingers through the crevices and around the convexities and surfaces of his slim, but still beautiful, body.

He, in turn, was looking at her, kneeling by the side of the tub. He loved her breasts. They were firm and full, yet the nipples were small and delicate with their café-au-lait pigmentation. He felt a surge of sexual desire, while at the same time being painfully aware that the desire was limited to his emotions, his eyes, his head, his sensate self. Lately it seemed as if some horrible cleavage had occurred between the thinking and feeling self, and his genital apparatus.

Sex had been difficult for them for some time. The pain of the sudden motions could be unbearable. He recalled that awful time when in a moment of passion he turned a damaged limb under him and, despite himself, had screamed. She responded with such guilt, such horror, that for weeks she would not touch him, even when he desperately longed for sexual contact. Later she would only allow him to lie passively while she masturbated or sucked him to orgasm, eschewing any gratification for herself. He supposed she must masturbate alone—and he longed for the former days when his capacity to arouse her to extravagant and uncontrolled passion was the most joyous aspect of their sexual union. Then for a few months all sexual desire seemed to have left him. Now the desire was returning but not the erection. What, he wondered, was desire? The longing was there; the wish was there; but the passion which converted anticipation into preparedness seemed totally absent.

"Stop ogling me," she said with a mock sternness, pleased at the obvious pleasure he got in seeing her near-naked body.

"Close your eyes and relax."

She picked up the soap, rubbed it through her fingers and began to lather and slowly move the slippery bar across the arch of his foot, gently and firmly massaging the foot, running her slippery fingers between his toes, slowly and softly manipulating each joint; being oh, so careful, aware of the potential tenderness and pain. She continued talking about the spate of publicity about Lincoln McAllister. He followed her injunction, closed his eyes and enjoyed the soft caress of her soapy fingers.

It was apparent to everyone, at this point, he thought, that Lincoln McAllister had captured the public imagination. He was the golden boy, elegant and refined, with an aura of sexuality that did not offend men while automatically captivating women. He could never remember a campaign in which it was a foregone conclusion this early as to who the party nominee would be. And not since Truman had there been a campaign on which the assumption that the incumbent was a loser was so widespread. He knew these things were planned well in advance. He was intrigued by the kind of orchestration that had obviously occurred. Lincoln McAllister's name was never out of the newspapers for more than three days. There were interviews with him; by friends; by people of distinction in a variety of fields in which his name was calculatedly introduced. Adam had always been captivated by craftsmanship and engineering, and he began to speculate how one manipulated the news. He had really not kept up with political news since his illness and realized that he rarely listened when Sarah talked politics. Politics had come to seem too ephemeral—too petty and compromising. He wanted meaning, not maneuvering, ideals, not pragmatics for his final hours. Nonetheless, Adam's mind seemed now to be pursuing some independent course. He liked that. It was precisely this kind of automatic stream of consciousness analysis that in the past had so often led to breakthroughs and solutions to problems in mathematics.

He had never been arrogant about his intellectual ability; he saw it as a gift. And, in a detached way, he was in awe of his own mind; respectful of it; enjoying "its" capacity to solve problems; to come to startling conclusions. For some reason his thoughts had now taken a darker tone. The concept of selling an image of a candidate and manipulating the media had automatically directed his thoughts to Roger Hilton. His disgust for Hilton was unalleviated by any touch of pity for his public humiliation, his defeat, his shattered career and his almost total isolation.

Yet it isn't really total isolation any more, Adam mused. No, it isn't. He began to sense a pattern—a new pattern.

Adam was now hooked into a problem. There was an arrangement, some facts that needed explaining; a parallelism that was beyond the statistics of mere chance, or that was at least likely to be beyond the statistics of chance. Yes, there was some connection, some relationship in a subtle way between Hilton and McAllister. In the exact time period that Lincoln McAllister was being promoted—with less drama and less exposure, there had been a quiet, shadow promotion of Roger Hilton. But how could that be? What possible connection could there be? McAllister was the opposite in personality and temperament of Hilton. Besides, he had broken with him early, and had come out of the scandals with his reputation intact. The men were of a different age. They represented antithetical attitudes towards government. It was part of McAllister's charm that one sensed that public exposure was always slightly painful to him. If there was a man for whom you could believe the presidency was seen as an act of service rather than self-interest, one would pick McAllister. There was an essential shyness that eschewed not only public adulation but even attention. He was private, but not secret—the opposite of the secretiveness of Hilton.

Adam's mind was now racing. There was a connection! In his mind he traced every reference to Hilton that had emerged in recent months, and that computerlike brain of his correlated the timing with the timing of McAllister's media campaign. His scientific intuition told him that this was not one of the chance events that plagued the statistician. No, this was a real connection. So here was a problem to be solved. A connection was established. What was the connection? What could be its answer?

But wait a minute, hadn't Sarah been talking about Hilton just a moment ago?

"What did you just say, honey?" he asked.

"I said that either I'm losing my taste for novels—a sure sign of encroaching middle age—or that no one knows how to write them anymore."

"No, I didn't mean that—I meant just before—about Roger Hilton."

"Just before? I don't believe you! Adam, that was five minutes ago!"

"I'm sorry. I must have dozed off."

"Like hell you did," she answered without anger. "You just turned me off, but I forgive you." And she leaned over and gently kissed him on the mouth.

He smiled, and brushed his cheek against hers, grateful for her good humor, her love and her unfailing patience with him.

"At any rate, all I said was that as sick as I am of seeing Lincoln McAllister in every paper and every magazine—I infinitely prefer his gorgeous face to that of our beloved former President. It's spooky how his name now keeps appearing. Everybody is beginning to wonder whether there might not be some direct connection between the two—but that seems absolutely paranoid. Two more distinct and antagonistic types couldn't be constructed. It makes no sense."

Everybody is beginning to wonder, Adam thought, incredulous. Everybody except stupid, horse's ass, shmuck boy genius me! I've been so involved in my narcissistic adolescent fantasy that I haven't seen what "everybody"—every fucking body—has known for months. Something is going on. Something important. And something involving that prick of pricks—Roger Hilton.

Sarah, meantime, continued her constant stream of chatter about daily events, her work, the market—knowing all the time that he was not listening, and, indeed, pleased that he wasn't. Her conversation was a form of music designed to soothe him, to bring him solace and surcease from pain, and the pleasure of being cared for. It was the cooing of a mother nursing, and the chatter that accompanied it; a kind of loving communication in which the sounds of words were more important than the meanings. She looked at his face; his eyes were closed and he was smiling. She wondered what he was thinking. Was he thinking of her? She looked at his body again. The radiation had removed almost all of the hair from the pubic area so that his genitals looked like those of a child. His penis, small, pink, and involuted, bobbed like a baby's bathtub toy. She leaned over tenderly and first kissed, and then gently nibbled the tip of his penis. He seemed totally unaware, lost in some deep reverie, some satisfying personal fantasy by the look on his face. She put one hand under the scrotum, cupping it softly, and with her other hand began to slowly massage the flaccid penis.

"It makes no sense," Sarah had said. But of course "it," whatever it is, never makes sense, Adam thought. Making sense is *our* responsibility. Data exists; cognitive minds gather and join that data until it does make sense, and, as usual, her instincts were right; there was a connection. There had to be a connection. Here was a problem that was both real and promising. And he, jerk that he was, was the last to be aware. But not any more, not now!

And the intellectual excitement of it caused him to stir in his bath. Sarah sensed a change in him, the flesh seemed to be coming alive under her fingertips. She assumed he was being aroused by her masturbating him, and therefore continued, hoping that the excitement this time might be translated to a physiological response. Not for herself any more; she was prepared to sacrifice her passion and sexual pleasure for his comforts. Her entire life was now committed to enriching the increasingly short interval that remained for Adam. She wanted the erection for his sake. She wanted Adam to enjoy the physical sense of being alive in those few months of life which might remain.

Rapidly he evaluated certain possibilities—his mind working like an automatic, independent mechanism, eliminating the most eccentric and statistically less sound probabilities until gradually one inescapable conclusion emerged. Lincoln McAllister, or his agents, was working with, or for, Roger Hilton. And yet the only likely solution was contradicted by the characters of the men involved. There were two parallel campaigns—matched and co-ordinated—of this he was sure. But even if matched and co-ordinated, whatever the purpose or motivation was—could anyone ever again be so naïve as to trust Roger Hilton? He doubted it. Well, let's assume they do not trust Hilton; they might, however, be underestimating the man. Perhaps someone felt that McAllister would be powerful enough to use and to control Hilton. But that would be a serious mistake. Nonetheless, it was an attractive hypothesis.

Then an intriguing alternate possibility occurred to Adam. Lincoln McAllister might be working for Roger Hilton without knowing it. That was a speculation worth evaluating.

Adam shook his head with mild annoyance at himself. He did not know enough about Roger Hilton. One essential ingredient in the problem was clouded by ignorance. He hated ignorance. He must study Roger Hilton. He must get to know him. He must solve this problem. One thing he did know—the man was evil—and totally self-serving. Roger Hilton would never serve any other man's purpose even if the other man thought so. My God, Adam wondered, could Roger Hilton be planning another thrust for power? Was it possible? Not really; not, at least, within the traditional political mechanisms. But when, he thought, had Hilton been stopped by the "traditional mechanism"—the legalities of the democratic system? He could contrive new political mechanisms. Did he have any power base? Who did he work with? The only one that remained loyal to him was that Irish fellow. What was his name? Duffy—something like that.

He must do some research; he needed more data. Hilton was evil. Hilton was an enemy worthy of attacking. Hilton was a dragon to be destroyed by the right knight.

A surge of excitement went through him. Here was a target; here was a direction; here was something to watch; and here was someone to destroy—if destroying was necessary. He felt alive in a way he had not for months. The excitement seemed to radiate through his mind, through his limbs, and he felt a throbbing in his groin. He looked down, shocked, to notice a tumescence in his phallus and a growing erection.

Sarah, who had been lost in her own thoughts, at this point experienced the emerging surge of power in the shaft of the no longer flaccid penis held in her hand. She felt the tightening in his scrotum, the pull of the testicles against her fingers, with the emergence of the full erection. She more firmly began manipulating his penis, while gently withdrawing the other hand out from under his buttocks. She struggled to pull off her shorts with her free hand. Now, completely naked, she entered the bathtub, kneeling and facing the supine boy. She noticed that his white body now seemed to have a rosier color, and the tiny nipples had contracted and firmed. She gently guided his penis into her vagina, and then placed both of her hands under his buttocks and slowly and gently, rhythmically pulled him closer into her, back and forth. Her hands, kneading and guiding his buttocks, began to tremble as her excitement mounted. It's like the first time, she thought, the first time, the first time, the only time. She heard a quiet groaning and, not sure whether it was her or him, she climaxed almost immediately. She wanted more—and still more—and all sense of time was erased as she gently straddled the now completely alive body of her lover. For Adam was once again her lover, slowly and gently continuing the thrusting, pulsating rhythm until she felt a spasm in the body beneath her as Adam ejaculated, crying out with a sound more of joy than a signal of release.

Chapter X

November—eight months before the convention

> James Doyle announced today that Roger Hilton would be renting space in the Wentworth Building. The purposes of establishing the office are to co-ordinate the ex-President's increasing involvement in cultural and philanthropic activities. (*The Wall Street Journal*)

Billyboy Haywood had been surprised to receive the call from Adam Haas. It had been over two years since he had heard from him. Nonetheless, when Adam asked if they could meet, the answer was an immediate yes—as it always would be. Billyboy was not one to forget favors. Adam Haas, young and innocent as he was, had been a mentor and, as unsuitable as it might seem, in that one critical year at Columbia, was like a father to him who had never known a father.

No one knew for sure whether this was his christened name, but Billyboy, or BB to his buddies, was all he remembered since childhood. Billyboy was one of the few poor Harlem black street kids of his generation who had managed to fight his way into the white establishment, or at least partway into the system.

Abandoned by his father shortly after his birth, he was raised with a progression of male surrogates who passed in and out of the household. Most of them sullen and indifferent; some malicious or brutal; and occasionally a concerned, affectionate man, with whom the boy could form an attachment—and whose leaving would cause Billyboy more pain than the cruelty and beatings of the others. His mother was psychotic and totally incompetent at anything except disastrous involvements mostly with brutes, leading to intermittent psychotic episodes and pregnancies. He was raised (and saved) by a loving grandmother, an extraordinary woman of great strength and dignity. She did other people's cleaning during the day and her daughter's at night. She raised Billyboy along with an assorted collection of step-siblings and half-siblings and foster children.

He grew up streetwise, lean and tough, but with one bewildering contradiction. He was possessed of a natural mathematical genius, which emerged despite a total lack of academic discipline. This mathematical aptitude, like an exotic flower growing in a cement sidewalk, was so ludicrously and paradoxically manifest that even the weary and jaded public school teachers could not avoid recognizing it. It was to become the link that would join two such unlikely backgrounds as those of Billyboy and Adam into a shared future.

From the beginning he was seduced, coddled and cajoled by an academic system that saw him as a potential star, with enormous promotional ability. Had he been taller he would have ignored his mathematical talent. He had the skills of a superb basketball player, but at just five nine he knew there was unlikely to be much future for him, and he eventually began to see mathematics as an alternative way out of the ghetto. Yet ghetto life was not all negative; he was stimulated by the push and shove of competing passions; the energy and excitement of the streets; the quick fixes and the slow dreams. The street life in Harlem excited and held him. A glib tongue, fast mind and a powerful body with natural athletic ability gained him access to the Harlem establishment of numbers and fences; of pimps and dope.

Except in mathematics, he was a diffident and not altogether successful student. He had little patience with the learning process—and succeeded only with that which came effortlessly. As a teen-ager he had been picked up two or three times by the police but managed to avoid being arrested. By the time he was fifteen, he was making two hundred dollars a week running numbers, and at the same time, encouraged by a high school teacher, he was studying mechanics and probability. At sixteen he was accepted at Columbia College as a special student in the Department of Mathematics. It was here that he met Adam. Adam, unsophisticated about the complexities of what went into a man like Haywood, saw him as naturally following in his own footsteps and encouraged him to go into a doctoral program.

He started the program at Columbia, but after achieving his master's degree, seemed to backslide. He lacked the discipline or, perhaps, just the interest to continue. Adam and he remained friends and confidants, and it was Adam who suggested that the world of business could also use mathematicians, that his choice wasn't the narrow one of street or college.

Billyboy took the advice, and found the direct experience in the problem-solving world of commerce a compromise he could enjoy. He now worked for IBM. Although he still found excitement in the world of the street and occasionally moved an easy buck with his old friends, he avoided the dangerous and grossly illegal, and Adam, when cognizant of these forays, had the insight to recognize that this was part of a process; that in a sense he was going through his social adolescence on the way to becoming a solid member of the black bourgeoisie.

Lately Billyboy had begun to think in terms of politics. He recognized that up to that point sheer luck had allowed him to have a totally clean record. In the last six months he had become more careful. For a middle-class, educated black, there were opportunities for power in the world of black, or even white, politics. Here was another game, as interesting and dramatic as the streets, to supplement the regularity of middle-class life, which would always have the unpalatable and doughy quality of monotony.

He hadn't been around the campus for over two years and found it amusing that Adam had wanted to meet him at the old hangout. He crossed Broadway, walked down past West 114th Street and entered the West End Bar. Walking through the dark bar area at the entrance he caught a glimpse of Adam's blond hair from the rear. He was wearing a ludicrous baseball cap, and he noticed that the hair trailed behind much longer than was Adam's former taste. He was sitting up on the platform area at the far end of the restaurant. He stopped, shocked at the image of frailty. My God, he thought, he's half the size he used to be. He then noticed the glint of light off the aluminum Canadian crutches. He had known that he was ill; Adam didn't talk about it, but the scuttlebutt around an academic community had made it clear that he had a terminal illness, and word had leaked back to Billyboy from mutual friends. "Terminal illness" was a vague phrase whose meaning Billyboy had simply not absorbed—or had not wished to. One look changed all that. He now knew what it meant. Instantly he was aware that Adam was dying, really dying. Old men die, he thought; tough, prematurely old black men die; even black children die. But rich, blond, clean white boys are supposed to grow into dignified and powerful old men. He was upset.

Adam, looking around impatiently, caught BB's eyes. Immediately Billyboy's expression changed. The anguish for his friend was erased as he slipped into a grin, a jive walk and the hipster talk with which he always first greeted Adam.

"Who dat dude sittin der?" he said. "Do I know he?"

Adam broke into a grin, slapped the hand offered to him, and said, "BB, oh, BB, do I need you!"

"Why, who you want killed, brother? Just give me the man's name and I'll slip him the black spot."

"For God's sake, BB, not so loud. We're in a fucking public place."

Billyboy was confused. Of course, he was jiving his friend but the look of anxiety that crossed Adam's face could only mean . . . he took me literally. Christ, I think he took me literally!

"Adam," he said, all traces of the phony patois disappearing with the new recognition. "What the hell are you talking about?"

"Oh, God, BB," Adam sighed. "I'd thought we'd have

a half hour over a couple of beers and I could have the decent politeness to let you fill me in on your life, your current sexual conquests, your progress on the way to becoming the first black billionaire President of the United States, and instead I blew it. I start right in with my idiot life, my selfish needs—and...oh, shit. Maybe it's just as well. I suppose you know I'm dying, BB. I don't want to talk about it though. I don't really need sympathy; that's not why I'm telling you. I'm telling you only because everything is condensed when you're dying. I don't have time for niceties and proprieties. I don't have time to plan a retirement. I don't even have time to plan a trip to Europe next summer. I don't know if I'll be here next summer.

"BB, I've gone from walking with difficulty, to walking with a cane, to walking with crutches, and I'm going to ask you to leave before you see me try that. I'm walking with crutches because I don't have the guts to be in a wheelchair where I really belong. Because I've got this stupid pride. I'd rather die with the pain than meet you in a wheelchair. I won't even let you see me with the crutches because I look like a freaky animal swinging around, and because I'm immature and because I'm still vain. But I don't have time, BB, for politeness, preliminaries, and so maybe it's just as well.

"I've got to get help for the one thing I still want to do. The one thing I must do before I die. And I know just how to do it, BB. *I know how to do it!* But I need some things. And what I need, any kid in the streets can get; but sophisticated Adam Haas hasn't a clue as to how to get."

"You need dope, is that it? For the pain, I mean. For God's sake, Adam, won't the doctor give it to you? I'll get you the shit. I swear it, just ask me. Whatever you need, I can get."

"No, I don't need dope. I've got good doctors. They'll give me as much as I want, or as much as I need. It's I who resist it. I don't want to die like an animal in pain, but I also don't want to die like a vegetable. BB, I want to do something! If not with my life, at least then with my death. There's something I've got to do. I've got to take someone out."

"Wha chou say. Take someone out!" he said, slipping into his street accent again.

"I mean what you mean when you say 'take someone out.' There is someone evil, and I think I may have to destroy him. Don't ask any more. I don't want you to know any more. I swear by the God that you believe in, and I don't, that I will not hurt anyone innocent; that I will not do anything that will offend you. Already I feel like a rat. I know that you've been walking a wire—and are finally safe on the right side—and now I'm asking you to do something illegal for me. And I hate myself for it. All the hard part of my planning is done but I'm so frustrated because the kind of thing that any fourteen-year-old punk in Harlem can get, I can't. And it could keep me from doing the one thing left for me to do."

He was now rambling and BB noticed him beginning to choke up, and thought, My God, he's going to start crying now, and if he does, then I'll start crying and I can't stand it.

"Hell, Adam, if a fourteen-year-old from Harlem can do it, certainly a smart twenty-two-year-old like me can do it. Don't get yourself worked up. What the hell is it? Just tell me. Tell me the plan. I got strong arms and strong legs, which you don't. I'll work with you."

"I don't want you to work with me!" said Adam with anger in his voice. "I'm mad enough at myself, having you an accomplice at all. I don't want you to be hurt. I want you to have the kind of life I can't. I want you to get out of all the shit you're still half playing around with. I want you to get married and have kids. I want you to do good work. I want you to grow old. I want you to grow old and respectable, because I can't. But first, I'm going to have to ask you to put all that at risk. I hate to ask it. And I half want you to say no, because if you got in trouble because of me I'd just die."

On hearing his last words he burst out laughing. "It's funny how you say that, and normally it has no meaning. What I mean is that I couldn't die in peace if in my dying I hurt you."

"Jesus Christ, Adam, tell me what it's all about."

"No, BB, I don't want to tell you. I want you to do

something as an act of faith in me. I don't want you to know anything, not because I don't trust you, but because I don't want you in this. I don't want your help, and I'm not confident I could resist your help if you offered it to me.

"I'm going to tell you what I need. I'm going to ask you once. I don't want you to talk. I want you to nod your head yes or no. Yes will mean you'll try—I know you can't guarantee delivery. No will mean you're the smart man I think you are."

Adam laughed. "This is the silliest position I've ever been in. I'm praying you'll say no, although with all my heart I want you to say yes. I really am a selfish bastard doing this to you. Anyway, no more talk. I'm going to tell you what I want. Just use your head one way or the other and then there's a handshake and good-by. If it's yes, you can call me and tell me whether you're able to get the stuff or not. If it's no, I still want to see you before—well, you know."

"Jesus," said Billyboy with a look of mixed disbelief and mounting anxiety. "You sure do make this sound mysterious. Go ahead already and ask the damn favor."

"Okay," said Adam. "Here's what I want from you. Two hand grenades. I have no technical knowledge of the new ones, so I can't be specific, but the lightest weight possible to be effective. One automatic weapon, preferably the Israeli Uzi or if not available, the German G-3; if you know of an even lighter-weight automatic rifle, all the better. And, of course, ammo for the rifle."

He stopped abruptly with no explanations and the two men sat for a moment just staring into each other's eyes across the table in the dimly lit bar.

Haywood thought, I should be laughing now. This is a very funny conversation. I should be laughing.

But he knew Adam and he didn't make jokes. Haywood felt cold, and shaky. The sweat broke out on his forehead. What in hell is all this? What can I do? What am I supposed to do? Time was passing, and he knew there was only one thing he could do. He tightly nodded his head, yes.

Adam extended his hand. Billyboy got up, went behind his chair and put his arms around him in a gentle bear hug. The tears were coming now, but Adam couldn't see.

"Please go now, BB. I want you to leave before I do. I don't want you to see me walking out of here with these things."

Without another word, Billyboy Haywood turned around and walked out of the bar.

Chapter XI

December—seven months before the convention

> Elizabeth Hilton was named honorary chairperson of the International Cancer Society's yearly fund-raising ball. Mrs. Hilton said she was honored to serve so worthy a cause. (Associated Press release)

Moss realized he had not been listening, and was annoyed with himself. Damn it, Judge Shaffer was paying enough for these sessions, he thought, and was entitled, at minimum, to his full attention. Of course, every analyst—every day of his life—would find moments of distraction, but Moss felt these lapses were occurring more frequently, and inevitably they were related to Adam. Peter had been thinking of the session to follow—and felt guilty. Not that the judge would have said anything that Peter had not heard from him before. He was in the closing phases of a successful analysis; it had been months, perhaps years, since any "new" insights had emerged. For the most part, analysis, anyway, was "working through"—the constant relearning of old problems in new contexts that gradually eroded neurotic structures and helped build new, more adaptive patterns. Still, he was Moss's patient, and this was his hour.

He focused his attention for the last ten minutes and terminated the hour pleased with the very real changes in Judge Shaffer, not always predictable in a man his age.

Moss opened the door leading from his consultation room to the waiting room, escorting the judge out, and noticed the attractive blond woman perched on the very edge of the couch. Only after he heard the click that indicated the judge had shut the door leading out of the office, did he turn to face her.

"Ms. Pedersen?" he asked with a smile, offering her his hand. She rose, shook hands with him, and he ushered her into the office, gesturing her to sit in a small armchair situated in tandem to the one he now sat in.

"I'm so grateful you agreed to see me, Doctor," said Sarah.

Peter Moss was always amazed to see how different real life individuals were from his fantasy conjectures. After all, he knew Sarah Pedersen almost as well as any of his patients, and better than most of his acquaintances and colleagues. Adam's analysis was filled with talk of Sarah. He knew her tastes in literature and music, details of her body, the intimacies of her sexual behavior, the idiosyncrasies and private fantasies—in fact all of the details that make for real knowing. And yet, once again, he was intrigued to rediscover that the visual presence of a person added an unknown dimension, and made all of the other facts synthesize into a whole that was inevitably different from the sum of the imagined parts.

The Sarah Pedersen he saw was not the same as, although sister to, the Sarah Pedersen that Adam described. What was different? She was stronger and younger. He smiled inwardly. Of course. A thirty-three-year-old woman is a mature, older woman to a twenty-two-year-old boy and a "girl" to a fifty-year-old man. He liked what he saw. She was not pretty, but she was a beautiful woman. There was real character in her face that he guessed would become even more beautiful as she would get older. Peter's thoughts were interrupted by her statement, and he immediately asked, "Does Adam know you are here?"

"No, he doesn't," she replied.

He sighed audibly. Normally he would not have agreed to see her without first discussing it with Adam and receiving his permission, but she had called just an hour and a half before with a note of such urgency in her voice, and since he had the cancellation he could not refuse her. It was characteristic of this treatment, he thought, that all the rules were gradually being broken, and he realized at that point how much the rules were designed for the protection of the analyst, as well as the patient.

"You understand, of course," he said, "that I will have to discuss everything we say with Adam."

"Of course. I know that. Under ordinary circumstances, I would never have considered coming to you without first asking his permission. Lord, in the past he had asked me to come, *wanting* me to meet you; wanting you to see me. In the old days I didn't come because"—she blushed as she said this—"he saw me as such a prize. I was afraid for you to see that *this* particular Dante's Beatrice was just plain old Jane. I wanted you to see me through his eyes. I've never been beautiful, and I relished the fact that through Adam, not just one, but at least two people would see me that way.

"Later on," she continued, "there were times when he wanted me to come, thinking that I could amplify certain things about our relationship; but by then I didn't want to come because I was afraid. I thought I would feel naked in your presence. There was so much that I knew Adam had discussed about us that one doesn't normally discuss. To meet a stranger who had 'seen' me naked was something I was not sure I could face. Funny, now that I'm here I'm not embarrassed. Perhaps I'm too frightened. I don't think so. I don't feel guilty either, although I'm usually a person with overwhelming guilts even for small transgressions. And certainly, normally, I would never do something behind

Adam's back. I feel like a spy betraying him, turning him over to the authorities. But then, you're not the authorities. You're his ally. At least, Adam has explained it to me that way, that the analytic situation is sacrosanct, like the confessional; that you can tell an analyst anything without fear of exposure, betrayal or even judgment or condemnation."

Moss began to feel uncomfortable and mumbled, "Well, not exactly. There are limits even to that."

"But sort of," Sarah continued. "I used to be jealous of you. He leaned on you so. He adored you so. Why do I speak of this in the past tense? Of course he still does. I speak of everything in terms of Adam in the past tense. Am I preparing myself for his death? Why do I find all the rules changed? Why am I, whom he trusts so, betraying him to another person, whom he also trusts so? Who may in turn also betray him? Why am I behaving in a way so atypical? It is death that is doing this to us. It is death that is changing the rules. Everything is different. 'Of all the world's wonders which is the most wonderful?' the Bhagavad Gita asks, and answers, 'That each man though he sees others dying about him never believes that he himself will die.' I would never believe it, would you, Doctor?"

She did not wait for an answer but continued the monologue. The rush of words suggested how long she had waited to share this information with someone even though she had yet to come to the point of her visit.

Peter Moss recognized her urgency, her need, and allowed her to continue uninterrupted.

"But Adam is different," she continued. "He does believe he is going to die. He is living for his death. It is I who cannot bear it. It is I who find myself denying it in a hundred different ways. Only in my speech am I betrayed. Only in the constant presence of the past tense; in the slips of the tongue; in the inability to visualize existence in the years ahead; in the tricks of my mind, do I know that somewhere in me there is an awareness that he will die.

"But," she continued, repeating herself, "he lives for his death. He's planning it. It's supposed to be healthy,

I understand. It's the new fashion, isn't it? I don't agree. I want to pretend that I will never die. I want to go out kicking and screaming and saying, 'Too soon, too soon, too soon'; even when I'm ninety. Maybe I will feel differently after Adam's..."

She paused. "I was going to say demise. Would you believe it, a priggish word like that? I could not bring myself—I will not bring myself—to use the honest word 'death' in relationship to Adam. What in God's name is happening to me?"

She then started giggling. "Oh, Doctor, what a fool I am! What a narcissistic fool. That is the chic new word, is it not?" she said, catching the smile on Moss's face.

"Here I am, talking about myself, *myself*. Is there something about this room? Is there something about your manner which does that to people? I had no intention of going on like this. I am not normally a chatterbox."

"Aren't you?" he asked.

She laughed. "My God, I forgot to whom I was talking. But the truth is, Doctor, I am not, except with Adam. There is something about our relationship that brings it out. I know that he likes me to talk, and so I do. I do everything to please him. But I am so frightened."

Moss wondered whether to reassure her. She was talking now as though she were in a therapeutic session—almost in free association. He sensed that at this point catharsis was more useful for her. Besides—besides, how could he reassure her? It was he, he realized, who was looking for reassurance from her!

"You know of course that he has been determined to find some way to put his death to use. He is an incredible researcher. He has spent the last two months doing nothing but reading up on Roger Hilton and Lincoln McAllister. But primarily Roger Hilton. He is obsessed with the man and what concerns me is that Adam has never been paranoid."

She interrupted herself. "I'm sorry for using the word. I'm not exactly sure what it means. What I really mean is, conspiratorial. But he is convinced from his readings that somehow or other there is a relationship between McAllister's obvious campaign for the presidency and the resurgence of public acceptance of Roger Hilton."

Adam was not paranoid; of that Moss was convinced. But there was something askew. Something that did not fit. It was the total implausibility of Adam's scheming. Adam was nothing if not rational. Illogicality pained him aesthetically. Adam could be naïve, foolish, romantic—but not paranoid and not irrational.

"Have you noticed, Doctor—I'm sure you must have—Hilton's name is beginning to crop up at social events and public meetings; groups are forming to vindicate him; the heated attack on the Korean scandal, the Chilean affair, the embezzlements of the General Services Administration—all these are used to emphasize how minimal Hilton's offense was. I sense it socially. People are beginning to feel sorry for the man. People are beginning to feel that he has paid his dues.

"But I'm sure he has discussed all of this with you. You know too, then, that he has come to the conclusion that Hilton is planning to return to political power. He doesn't know how yet, but he is convinced that Hilton sees McAllister as his bridge back to more than respectability. I keep telling him that McAllister doesn't impress me as that kind of person, and that part does disturb him. Because McAllister probably is a decent person, albeit somewhat shallow, if one can accept the validity of his public image.

"At any rate, he hates Hilton with a passion and he keeps saying, 'He's smart enough to learn from his last mistakes. This time the takeover will be complete. The man must be stopped and I will stop him.'"

"Yes, he has discussed this with me," Peter Moss said reassuringly. "But he won't do it. He can't do it. He can't psychologically or physically, for that matter. I've let him talk because he needs some occupation beyond his own personal tragedy. I'm almost grateful for anything that takes him away from the subject of his own death. I do agree with you that there is an obsessive quality to it, but there is a large gap between fantasy and reality and what we..."

Sarah interrupted, "He has just made a major step to bridge that gap."

"What do you mean?" Moss responded, startled.

"The other day a friend of his showed up with a strange delivery. It was a heavy enough package that Adam couldn't handle it and had the friend place it in the bedroom. When I asked him what it was he said that this was one case where it would be best if I respected his privacy. He wanted me not to investigate the contents of the box.

"He's such a child." She laughed, despite her patent anxiety. "Our relationship is too far gone for that. He knows me well enough to know that, particularly after a statement like that, my curiosity would almost demand I look.

"I wonder now, did he really want me to look? Was that also part of the plan? Was he testing me? Oh, Lord, now I'm thinking in a conspiratorial way. Here I am talking about him to his analyst, behind his back, so to speak, and I'm accusing him of manipulating me.

"What is there about death that seems to change all the rules? Or maybe it isn't death. Maybe it's us, our times. Trust is in such rare supply. And then, again, I suppose it isn't even trust, it's all this question of divided loyalties, of who we are, of who owns us, of which master we are serving at which time. I betray him—and you betray him—because we love him and because we are concerned for him. Poor Judas. I understand him better now."

Moss tried not to wince at her last statements. Whose agent was he? Was he protecting Adam, society, his own reputation, his own conscience? Who knew where right was in a mess like this? He did not like the direction things were going with Adam and he had no confidence in his own capacity to control events. Worse, he had no confidence in his capacity to know what the decent, proper, right action should be.

"You still haven't told me what was in the box," he said.

"Well, I don't know much about this stuff, but any idiot can recognize what seemed to me rounds of ammunition, one of those little submachine guns that you always see in terrorist movies, and, if I'm not mistaken, a couple of hand grenades. Jesus Christ, it looked like a toy bin except that everything weighed a ton and it had that oily, new machinery quality that signifies the real thing."

"Did you confront him about this?" asked Moss.

"I haven't had time. He was out this morning when I looked and the first thing I thought of was calling you. Did he discuss it with you, Doctor? That is what concerns me. I know he has in the past always trusted you implicitly, and I took comfort in that knowledge that, somehow, someone else was in control besides me. I thought you could convince him to be reasonable. Did he tell you?"

"No, he didn't, but on the other hand, as you say, he just got it and I have not seen him since Monday. We do have an appointment tomorrow morning. So he really hasn't had time to discuss it with me," he said without completely reassuring himself or her.

"These things didn't just arrive. You don't stop at the local A&P and pick them up, or even have them delivered. He made arrangements, plans, contacts. It must have been going on for weeks. I know he keeps things from me—but I thought you were the safety valve. You are the one he supposedly tells everything. Don't tell me you had no idea of this. For God's sake, Doctor, don't tell me he didn't discuss any of this with you."

"I'm afraid he did not," he responded slowly. "He certainly did not"—the full implication of her statement finally settling in.

93

Chapter XII

January—six months before the convention

> The Cincinnati Trust Co. announced today the election of Roger Hilton to its Board of Directors. (Cincinnati *Enquirer*)

"What do you mean, it never came to mind?" Peter Moss asked, allowing a note of incredulity to slip into his voice.

"I mean, Doctor, precisely what I said," Adam responded with anger and mild sarcasm. "It literally never came to mind, at least not while I was here. I save these hours for important things. Details have never been important to me. You're a psychoanalyst; details are important to you. I'm a mathematician; it's concepts that concern me. I let the engineers work out the details. I had a problem which required a major solution. The problem wasn't getting arms. Every punk kid in the city can get a 'piece.' Why the hell should I think with my middle-class connections and my middle-class money, that I couldn't buy dynamite, explosives or whatever I needed. I certainly told you I once was thinking of building an atomic bomb."

"You sure did," Moss said. "And don't think it didn't scare the hell out of me."

"You ought not be frightened of anything I do. I'm not psychotic. I'm not a fool. I'm not impetuous. Why do I have to tell you these things at this late stage? You, who are supposed to know me better than anyone else? You annoy me when you accuse me of deceiving you. The purchase of the weaponry never seemed a problem, therefore I never discussed it with you. The problem was: what to do with my death, how to make a statement, how to leave a mark, how to take those last moments of unexpected energy stored in this dying animal and use it for some purpose?

"I've told you constantly—and it's the one thing you refuse to hear—that you cannot do your usual 'thing' with me. You cannot help me to live a better life. You can only help me to die properly. I have too little life left to worry about. Less now than ever."

"What do you mean?"

"I've stopped all treatment. All of it. The chemotherapy, the radiation, all of it."

"With Dr. Castle's approval?"

"Of course not with the approval of that asshole," Adam said bitterly, the language of the boy breaking through with his anger. "He would continue treating my fucking disease even after I was dead, if that were allowed. But I know you are different. You are concerned with me, not my cancer. I am not just a patient. I'm the son you never had—even if you won't admit it. At least you will admit to being my friend. Come on, it won't hurt—tell me you really like me."

Peter grinned and shook his head.

"So don't get angry with me," Adam continued, his own anger abating. "I can't stand the feeling you don't love me. Understand. Understand why I want some purpose in my death. I want to attach some sense to this senseless thing that's happening to me. What can I do? I'm not content to simply sign my parts away. First of all, they're no damn good, decimated with sarcoma. So I can't even have that privilege. I leveled with you. I told you I wanted to kill Roger Hilton, and I told you why. You felt my ideas were preposterous. Maybe they are. If events prove them to be preposterous, or if you convince me, or, which is more likely than the other two, if I die before I have an opportunity to execute my plans, I will not assassinate him. Otherwise I intend to. I'm now working on the methods. Just so you don't think I'm trying to deceive you I'll tell you this—if I thought some fucking blowdart, like in a goddamn Tarzan movie, would kill him, I wouldn't worry about finding the blowdart or the poison—I would still start by going to the library and researching the poison. I would then manufacture or purchase the poison, and set the plan for logical and foolproof delivery. Then and only then would I attend to the trivial problem of finding a blowdart, because I'm sure that somewhere in the black hole of Harlem, there's a blowdart for sale to anybody who's got the bread."

Adam started smiling at the picture of the blowdart and he was pleased to notice simultaneously a grin spreading across the face of Peter Moss.

He was no longer lying on the couch; getting on and off was simply too painful. He sat on the chair opposite Moss, and Moss shoved over the footstool which normally he used during analytic hours, so that the boy would have some support for his knees. Mercifully, the bone tumor seemed to avoid the upper limbs, although there were signs of spread into the pelvis and both lower legs.

Again, it was sheer luck (he had seen the X-rays) that he had not yet fractured one of the long bones of the left leg. It was now so riddled with cancer.

"I like this," said Adam.

"You like what?"

"We had an argument or something close to it. I don't think that's ever happened before. It's a sign of love, you know. Analysts don't argue with their patients. Parents do with their children. You lost your professional cool, Doctor."

Moss did not answer but he felt uncomfortable and wondered if he were blushing. Adam was right, of course. He was a father of a wayward child. Twelve years of schooling, he thought, four years of college, four years of medical school, a year of internship, three years of psychoanalytic training, and he might as well have been an amateur. Perhaps that was too extreme. He was more disciplined than any amateur, yet his emotions *were* apparent, and he *was* involved. There was a peculiar kind of love, he thought. How perceptive of him. This vulnerable, tragic boy, like an optical lens, focused and magnified all of the emotions inherent in the psychoanalytic position to a burning intensity.

"So you see, Doctor, I didn't tell you the technical

details any more than a composer who would be in treatment with you would discuss the technical details of his orchestration. Of course he's going to mention his concerns about his composition and the nature of it to you, and his plans for its presentation, but the technical details wouldn't occur to him. These are just technical details."

"Well then, suppose you tell me"—Moss smiled—"about your box of 'technical details'; when the performance is to be; and who you've recruited for your army."

"You are looking at my army, Doctor. I believe in simplicity. I wanted the gun because a machine gun, an automatic rifle, seemed to me a logical weapon for an amateur. I wanted to know how heavy it was, and whether I could handle it. I wanted to know if I could engineer modifications on it and hide it. I wanted to know how to use it in case I needed it, but I never intended to use it. We mathematicians are always attracted to the simplest solutions—the one-page proof is always more elegant than the forty-page thesis. One looks for the least cumbersome, and the most direct solution to a problem. To me it seemed obvious—the hand grenade. I tried and tested the instrument. Any dummy can learn to use it and it's the traditional weapon for wasting one's own superiors in the armies."

"And what are you going to do with a hand grenade? Slip it into your victim's pocket?"

"What a lovely idea, Doctor. But now I can't use it, because your conscience would trouble you the rest of your life. You would have aided and abetted my crime. You know that Hilton is moving this month?"

"It's all over the papers. I couldn't have missed it," said Moss.

"Did you also notice those two little items, one announcing that he was taking a consultant's job with the Sino-American Amity Association?"

"No, I seem to have missed that."

"Did you also miss the second factor, that the Wentworth Foundation is going to make office space available for him at their headquarters in the city to facilitate his 'philanthropic endeavors.' And did you also notice that the YAF, those snotty, fascist, pubescent pimps, have invited him to be a keynote speaker at their spring meeting? My God, in another two years we will all be kissing his ass! Or worse: We'll all be eating out of his hands."

"These broad inferences," Moss interrupted. "These conjectures which may or may not be true are all granted a credence, a validity, which you would never have allowed in a more settled time of your existence. You are nothing if not a rational human being, Adam. Do not undermine that cornerstone of your character. Rationality is a rare commodity these days. Value your own. Do not destroy it. That would be tragic."

"Of course, Doctor, I know that all I have now is an intelligent hunch—but it is based on more research and more information than are worth relating to you in these expensive hours. You have not, after all, lowered your fees in deference to my tragic state."

"Never mind your tragic state." Moss smiled. "It is your flamboyant imagination that concerns me now."

"Well, as I was saying before I was interrupted—by the way, are you aware of how much talking you do in these hours? I used to beg for a few words, and treasure the crumbs of articulation dropped from the quiet of your reserve. We talk to each other now. I like that better. Is it still psychoanalysis?"

"No."

"I know. I'm trying to distract you, to make you feel guilty and to get you involved in a discussion. I will go on. What was I saying?"

"We were talking about the confusion of fact and conjecture. A fatal one for a serious thinker, particularly a scientist," Moss said.

"Of course," Adam continued. "Of course I am aware that so far I have no evidence. But since I know that my life will be incomplete, I indulge myself by operating on the assumption that my special project will be completed, and I make my plans accordingly. Then, when I have sufficient evidence to satisfy me—and I'm not a court of law; I do not need a demonstration of conclusive proof—then I can act.

"With Roger Hilton I do not make an assumption of innocence. He is guilty. If he died for no other reason than what he *wished* to do to this country, he would deserve to die. If he died for no other reason than what he *did* do to this country, it would be warranted. The fact that he is an impotent monster, if he is indeed impotent, makes his death unnecessary—but not necessarily unjustifiable. Were he a threat to the institutions of our country, his death would not only be just but necessary. My plan is contingent on the assumption that it will be both just and required."

"What plan? Are you going to machine-gun him to death on his estate in Briarcliff?"

"At this point in time," said Adam, "the machine gun is just a reserve. I don't know how I can handle that kind of equipment. But the lovely hand grenade— I could carry in my coat pocket. Indeed, I *have been* carrying it in my coat pocket. And if, as I sense will happen, he begins to return more and more to public life, someday in a public space an innocent, harmless, helpless cripple will be standing near him and will toss that hot potato of a grenade right into his lap."

"You don't even know what a grenade means!" Moss exploded. "I can't believe you're carrying one around with you!"

"Believe it," said Adam, pulling it out of his jacket pocket.

"Christ," said Moss. "Give me that goddamn thing."

"Like hell I will," said Adam, and carefully put it back in his pocket with a proprietary gesture of an adolescent boy pocketing his baseball.

"Well then, let me tell you something about grenades," said Moss. "That little gadget you have in your pocket has the explosive force not only to take Roger Hilton to hell but some innocent old lady passing by, or some schoolgirl and a priest who happened to be in the same public location with you. Grow up, Adam! This isn't cops and robbers. When that thing goes, the fragments can kill anybody in the vicinity. It can maim a great many people, and still leave your precious Roger Hilton intact and make him an even more heroic figure after an assassination attempt. Remember the transformation of public attitude about Governor John Connally. No, of course you don't. You're too young.

But surely you must remember the almost overnight change in the public awareness of George Wallace. You're going to end up making a goddamn hero of your villain."

Adam was interested. This was factual information. He needed more of it and it was something that had indeed occurred to him. He was now playing innocent.

"But what about all the stories out of the Korean War, of a soldier lobbing a grenade under a lieutenant's cot? You're not going to say those things didn't happen."

"Yes, of course they happened," said Moss. "And I personally am aware of at least one case, but the very close quarters under a bed helps to shield those around. Those fragments drive right through the bed and into the body of the person sleeping there. But even in those cases pieces of spring could be picked out of officers sharing the same barracks thirty feet away and fragments of the grenade, even when semi-smothered like that, can dangerously penetrate innocent bystanders.

"Surely you've seen enough movies and read enough war books to know that the only way to protect the crowd from a grenade about to go off is by that very act which alone is automatic guarantee of a Congressional Medal of Honor. Only if the individual literally smothers the grenade with his own body will it absorb the entire impact. The tissue, sinew, muscle, bone of an individual wrapped around the grenade will absorb its lethal fragments and he will be blown to smithereens and there is no way in hell you're going to get Roger Hilton to fall on a grenade, to smother it with his body, any more than you will get him to swallow it."

"Doctor," said Adam, "if there is a theoretical way; and if there is sufficient motivation—there is always a way to engineer it."

He paused for a moment, smiled and said: "And if there isn't, I've always got the automatic rifle."

Chapter XIII

February—five months before the convention

> Elizabeth Hilton was admitted today to the Harkness Pavilion at Columbia-Presbyterian Medical Center. A spokesman for the family said it was merely a routine checkup. (New York *Post*)

It was February and Peter Moss was suffering the late winter doldrums. By the end of February the New York winter became intolerable to him. He traditionally took a vacation the last week of the month. He liked the idea of leaving in February, spending a week in a tropical climate, and returning in March. God knows March could still be bitter and blustery—but for Moss it had the psychological feeling of spring. Never mind that more snow fell in March than in December—March was all potential and promise—and the lengthening of the days could almost be measured with each delayed sunset. He hated winter; he had no interest in winter sports, and the forced inactivity was almost an imprisonment.

It was still too early to garden but two giant oaks had been felled in severe storms that summer, and when told it would cost $600 to slice them up or $1,200 to cart them away, he elected the former. It was one thing to pay for something that added to your pleasure—it was outrageous to pay for a loss. He would miss those trees.

He had made the decision to install a wood-burning stove the following fall, and in the meantime splitting the three-foot slabs of oak into logs would be good exercise for the winter. He had been unprepared for the amount of work involved. The drier wood that he had split in the past popped deliciously with the hammering in of the first wedge. But the oak was still somewhat green, and the round pieces, often as much as four feet in diameter, required multiple sections. The wedges would get stuck in the wood and he found himself cursing—as much with frustration as with the ache in his shoulder and back muscles that had not had such demands made on them in years.

Still, in a perverse way, he enjoyed the activity. The physical effort conquered the cold he loathed, and the mechanical work allowed his mind to wander in a form of free association that had always released him from the specific worries of his practice and practical life. He did his best theoretical thinking while occupied with physical labor. This was how he did most of his writing. The free flow of ideas formed thoughts, arranged facts into syntheses and laid the groundwork for things that later would be placed on paper.

But once again, traditional methods were failing him. He was, almost predictably, occupied with Adam Haas and his last meeting. What could he make of that boy? How seriously should he take all this about assassinations? At first it was all so easy; it was part of the fantasy presented by every patient. In the unconscious of every man is murder and mayhem, rape and incest—a complete catalog of sins from Cain to the horrors of technological destruction. But rarely in his practice did violence intrude from the level of thought into action. How seriously should he take these fantasies of Adam?

At least three sets of facts needed balancing to determine the decision. First, were Adam's speculations even true? Of course he was correct in assuming an immense whitewashing of Roger Hilton was occurring. That now had to be obvious to everyone. But was it really calculation and plot, or simply the re-emergence of the conservative forces to re-establish their position and to reinstate one of their own kind. It did seem suspicious, however—and certainly beyond coincidence (he had to allow that)—that the process of reinstating respectability was moving so rapidly and seemed almost directly concurrent with the campaign for the nomination for President of Lincoln McAllister.

Supposing Adam were right up to this point; supposing he were correct, even at the most conspiratorial level, and that the two facts were linked, what then? There was no way that Peter could conceive of Hilton making the leap from social acceptance to political power. But it wasn't Peter that had to conceive of it, it was Adam. And Adam seemed convinced! He was disturbed by that. He respected his incredible intelligence—and, after all, he was not an ivory tower academic. He had worked in politics. He understood its machinations better than Peter himself. If Adam were convinced that Hilton was to be returned to power, then, by his somewhat warped attitudes, he had a legitimate target.

But even if condition one were met, what about conditions two and three? Could Adam actually commit an assassination? It was murder, after all. This gentle, intellectual, middle-class youth; the darling of three adoring sisters; the golden boy of elderly parents; cosseted, protected, indulged; this was not the stuff of a murderer. It did not make sense—psychologically it did not make sense to Moss—that someone like Adam could cold-bloodedly plan an assassination. Yet, Peter asked himself, what in God's name do I know about these things? The entire Red Brigade is probably recruited from just such middle-class boys. It's beyond my experience; beyond my expertise; it is the phenomenon of our times, and I am as alien to their thinking as to the mores of a Micronesian culture. Who am I to say that he could not do it? His generation and mine are separated by the kinds of events and horrors that shape new ways of thinking, new psychologies and, therefore, new capacities to act.

Peter began to get frightened by the direction of his thoughts. If Adam was serious, he had to notify the authorities. But what authorities? The police? The FBI? What would he present to them? Some vague confidences to which he had been entrusted—for God's sake, he had been entrusted with these confidences, he was a psychiatrist! And it was all totally undocumented, all hearsay. Would the police believe him? Would they not laugh him out of the station? And even if they did believe him, when they tracked down the potential murderer, what would they find—a helpless cripple. It was this third point that gave Peter the most relief from his ambivalence and anxiety. There was no way in hell someone so physically handicapped could all alone carry off an assassination. But why alone? What about accomplices? There was Sarah—strong, young, mobile. She could be his body, his legs, his tool. Yes, of course, he would be the brain planning the activity and she would exercise the plan. But that's preposterous, Peter realized. Adam would never even contemplate an assassination except (to use his phrase) to "give meaning to his death." Sarah was not dying and Adam would never destroy her potential for future happiness. He could never corrupt or damage her existence even for his most urgent needs. He loved her, and he protected those he loved.

The whole consideration constantly led in circles of contradictions. Every time he went at the problem he returned to the same inevitable position. Adam might plan all he wanted but there was nothing he could do. And yet? And yet this was not an ordinary man. This was Adam Haas. And somehow the circles of logic kept getting smaller and narrower, tighter and more constricted, until Peter felt himself suffocating in the bind. He could not bear the responsibility. He could not allow an assassination; but Adam Haas had, at most, another six to twelve months to live. It was his job to protect him, not society.

"It's hopeless, I'm right back to where I started from, where I always start from," he said out loud. He was startled at the sound of his own voice. Jesus, he thought, I better get back in the house before I lose my own rationality.

He came into the house, cleaned up and went to the library, where his wife, Ann, was reading. She put down her book, aware that he wanted to talk. She made some martinis on the rocks. They sipped in silence for a while. Then Moss began to talk, but not, to Ann's surprise, about Adam, but about his college days at

Harvard. He told her that since he would be in Washington on business, anyway, that Tuesday, he was going to call Skip and arrange for a lunch.

"Skip?" she said surprised. Skip was Peter's oldest friend, and, in a peculiar way, his closest. They had been college roommates and had formed the kind of attachment that is only formed among men when they are young. Skip at the time was having his problems with drinking and readjusting to the post-war world. If one could believe Peter on this, Skip never attended a class through that entire year and yet had a record which included as many As as Es, and little in between. When he could pull it off, he could pull it off brilliantly; otherwise he failed the course miserably. The nickname Skip was reverentially conferred on him by his classmates, in awesome acknowledgment of his total absence from classes.

Although the two men only shared the one year, Skip having moved on to get his doctorate somewhere in the Midwest, they had maintained the kind of deep friendship that requires little contact, yet could be drawn upon at times of crisis. When Skip's wife was desperately ill with what had been originally misdiagnosed as leukemia, the first person he called for consultation was Peter. They tended to talk once or twice a year on the phone—perfunctory, it seemed to Ann, almost smart-ass conversations that hid a close abiding friendship and respect. Why Skip, she mused, and why now, and why in relationship to his brooding about Adam?

"What did you say?" he asked.

"I didn't *say* anything. What I was thinking was, why Skip? And why now? He works for the Department of the Interior, doesn't he?"

"He used to, but not any more. I have never been quite clear when he was with the Interior, nor for that matter what he did. It obviously had something to do with security, and I never questioned him much. He moved around a lot—like a typical Washington bureaucrat. I have a number for him now. I think it's with Justice."

"Is he in Intelligence?" Ann asked.

Peter laughed. "I really don't know if Intelligence is the right word. I suppose that's one of the mysterious things; whatever the nature of the job is, it discourages inquiry. He has to be a major power in the security operations of the country. He has said as much. It's obvious that he doesn't want me to ask specifics, so I don't. Though he flits from one assignment to another, I have always suspected some permanent arrangement with the CIA."

"What's that got to do with Adam?" she asked.

"Nothing, I hope."

"Jesus, Peter, what is that supposed to mean? Are you worried that the boy is going to go out in some physical blaze? Has he gone bananas?"

"What kind of language is that for the wife of a psychiatrist?"

"For God's sake, Peter, don't play games with me. What is worrying you?"

He decided to lay the whole problem out for Ann; to tell her the entire story. What the hell—confidentiality was blown a dozen different ways and he needed her common sense. He told her the outline, leaving out only the specific references to names, such as that of Billyboy Haywood, although he did include the fact that Adam now was in possession of a machine gun and grenades. He told her his own reasoning; his very serious doubts as to whether Adam was physically able to handle the job. He told her everything.

Instead of getting the reassurance he expected, he became painfully aware of her mounting anxiety. She was not a person who frightened easily, and, somehow or other, her tension added a dimension of reality to the scheme. It seemed to tip the scale in the direction of fact rather than fantasy.

After a long pause she finally said, "You must do something, Peter."

"What can I do?"

"You cannot allow even the possibility of his taking the life of an innocent man."

"I suppose you're right," Peter said. "I know you're right."

He paused. "But," he murmured almost to himself.

"But what?" she said.

"But supposing it weren't an innocent person. Supposing it were someone who deserved to die. Supposing it were someone who ought to die."

"Jesus, Peter, I was wrong. It's you who are going bananas, not Adam. Who *deserves* to die? Who *ought* to die? Who is that pathetic boy, or you, for that matter, to decide such issues? Peter, you're scaring me."

Her anxiety decided him. He must act. He did not know how or when yet, but he would at least talk to Skip. Skip knew more about these things. He could perhaps guide him. Yes, he must call Skip tonight.

Chapter XIV

February—five months before the convention

> Tom Snyder announced that he would
> present a three-segment interview with
> ex-President Roger Hilton in June—one
> month before the convention. *(Variety)*

Peter Moss was so preoccupied that he was startled to notice that the cab had turned into Wisconsin Avenue and that the long, usually tedious ride from Bethesda, Maryland, was almost over. He was a consultant to the National Institute of Mental Health on problems of education and training in psychiatry and he made the trip to Washington with a reasonable degree of frequency. Usually he shuttled in with the attitude of a commuter rather than someone on a trip; certainly, it never seemed an occasion for socializing or entertaining. He had resolved to call Skip before coming—and then, somehow, decided against it. But just before leaving the NIMH he had made an impulsive call, and with the fortuitousness that characterized their relationship, managed to find him in. He had tried to keep any note of urgency out of his voice, merely suggesting that he wouldn't mind meeting him for a drink, to discuss "a few things that are troubling me." He was unsuccessful. There had always been a nonverbal communication between them that transcended the substance of their speech. Skip mentioned a small French restaurant tucked into a side street of Georgetown where they had met on at least two or three other occasions; it seemed to be a favorite of Skip's, and Peter liked it because it was away from the depressing pretentiousness of most of Washington's meeting places.

He wondered how much time Skip spent in Georgetown in relation to his other work. Where in the world did he work when not at the school, he wondered to himself? He had once asked Skip why they met there and it was passed off by some unconvincing reference to its proximity to the university. But how often was Skip at the school these days? He had the sense he was only an occasional lecturer. Someday he would have to find out. He wondered why Skip always seemed to prefer secluded or private places. Was it the fact that he was such a private person in general? Was it something about the nature of his job that demanded privacy? Well, after all, whatever that private job was, it was in an area that now concerned Moss and it was specifically in that professional capacity that Moss was meeting with him.

The cab pulled to a halt. He paid the cabdriver and went into the dark room. It was early, and except for a cluster around the bar the small restaurant was nearly empty. He walked through and saw Skip sitting at the table, sipping a glass of white wine. He smiled to himself. In the last twenty years Skip, who had had a severe drinking problem when he knew him in college, had limited himself to one glass of wine at dinner and one at lunch.

Skip, seeing him, put out his hand without rising and said, "Ahh, the distinguished author, teacher and New York Society shrink."

They shook hands, Peter closing his left hand over Skip's hand, firmly clenched in his own. There was so much genuine affection between them. He really would have liked to embrace him in a bear hug, but Skip's New England reserve was offended even by words of affection, let alone a demonstrative act. They sat looking at each other, exchanging small talk about wives and children, breaking into self-conscious grins over the foolish reminiscences of earlier days that punctuated their conversation. Peter ordered a second martini and noticed that Skip was still only a third of the way down his glass of wine.

Not until the martini arrived and the waiter had left did Peter bring himself to the purpose of the meeting.

"Before I start on the second drink and become totally inarticulate, I've got to get down to the business at hand."

"You mean this is not just a social visit we are having," Skip said with his usual irony.

"You know damn well it isn't. I need your advice."

"It's an honor to be an adviser to the man who is himself an adviser to some of the great of our time."

"It happens to be true, but how the hell would you know that?" asked Peter, laughing.

"We have our ways," said Skip.

There was something in the tone of the voice that made Peter look more intently at him. Did he mean that seriously? he wondered. But then Peter checked himself, thinking, I really am getting paranoid, seeing spooks even on the faces of friends.

"Skip," Peter started, "I've never asked you specifically what you do."

"I've never wanted you to ask. That's why you never asked."

"Well, I suppose I still don't need to know. I know it has something to do with security and intelligence and I assumed, knowing you, that it's at a reasonably high level. I need some advice on a theoretical case."

"Oh, my word," said Skip mockingly. "A theoretical case indeed! Like the people who come up to you with their theoretical cases of children on drugs, or problems with homosexuality in brothers and sons. That kind of 'theoretical' case?"

"For once in your life play dumb and let me call it

109

a theoretical case. Keep your thoughts to yourself. I don't want to get specific but let me sketch an outline. Supposing that a psychiatrist..."

"A 'theoretical' psychiatrist?" interjected Skip.

"Yes," laughed Peter. "A theoretical psychiatrist has a patient who is threatening to commit a violent act. The psychiatrist knows that he..." Peter was upset with himself. Already he had revealed the gender. He quickly covered, knowing it was useless.

"Supposing a patient has threatened to do an act of violence. The analyst knows the patient, as only an analyst can know an individual. In addition, the patient trusts the analyst completely and thoroughly, and, therefore, the analyst would have advance knowledge of any specific future behavior of the patient. It is the analyst's judgment that the threatened socially dangerous piece of behavior is only a fantasy—a necessary illusory game to occupy the patient during a difficult period of his life. On the other hand, there is always the possibility that the patient, because of the peculiar circumstances of his..."

He stumbled and hesitated, looking for some general way to describe the desperation of a dying person.

"Because of the," he continued awkwardly, "critical stage in the life of the patient, there is at least a possibility he might be forced to do something precipitous, and in that sense unchartertistic. In this case, the psychiatrist would be risking some social damage on the basis of a professional predictability which would not be as accurate as his normal capacity to predict— where the normal variables, that is, the traditional one of a standard patient's life, exist. He..."

"Stop, already," Skip said. "And spare me the 'ones' and 'conditions' and 'critical phases.' What in the world are you talking about? And how in the world do you expect me to give you any advice? I appreciate your respect for anonymity, but Lord, Peter, you're talking about psychological factors, complex interrelationships between people; do you really expect me to be able to fill in, between all those dots and vague generalizations and idiot sociology-type clichés, and come up with any kind of intelligent judgment? Why don't you just have your pretend discussion with a pretend friend, and come to whatever conclusions you wish to come to? I'm not fool enough to give you any advice on such laundered data as you feel appropriate to offer me."

"Of course, you're right," Peter said soberly. "I don't know what's happened to me. I'm so distrustful—and then, I'm not used to talking about my patients. What may have started as training, is now habit. I feel guilty talking about my patient—like some damned undisciplined gossip. I'm like a right-handed man trying to do things left-handed. I'm self-conscious and awkward, and worse, unsure, even as I talk to you, as to my purposes, let alone my justifications—and I don't like it. Be patient for a while. Perhaps I'd better have the second drink."

He took a long, stiff sip of the martini. He had never been a drinker, and were he wise, he would have limited himself to one. He knew perfectly well that by the end of the second martini he would be high. Perhaps, he thought, he needed that to give him the rationalization ("after all, I was drunk at the time") to continue with his story.

"Let me start over. I have a young man in treatment who is in a desperate state. He is contemplating assassinating a public figure. For specific reasons which I will not go into, I know him incapable of carrying out the act. And here you must take my word for it. I am not just talking about a character judgment, I mean that he is *physically*, as well as psychologically, incapable of carrying out the specific act of assassination he has in mind.

"Yet, like everything else in life, there is no absolute predictability. If I have a patient who is a suicide risk, I will carry it to a point where my self-confidence is stretched to its thinnest, because I know unnecessary hospitalization will slow recovery. I increase the connections between me and the patient as an alternative. Even then, there is a slight risk, although, thank God, I have not lost a patient that way yet.

"But there I am balancing the good of the patient against a potential harm to the same patient. Here, the risk is not to the patient, himself. I have never before had a patient who was threatening another person. Perhaps, because—you were of course right—I see upper middle-class people, establishment figures. The more successful I am, the higher my fees, the more I approximate the society doctor so often criticized in my profession. I'm saved, I suppose, by the fact that I teach at a university and therefore am constantly involved with students and their friends. That is my balance.

"And still, even in the heart of the radicalism of the sixties, when I was sitting on some pretty antsy stuff, I was never faced with this specific situation of someone about to..."

He heard what he was about to say and was shocked. Was it his unconscious speaking directly? He shook off the thought and said, "I'm sorry. I was saying I have never before been involved with someone who talked so directly about a specific act of violence."

Skip did not like what he was hearing. He must not allow his concern to show. Peter was a risk-taker, and he knew that his self-confidence as a therapist bordered on arrogance.

"When you say 'a specific act of violence,' do you mean that the target is already selected or do you mean more than that?" Skip asked.

"I'm afraid I mean more than that," Peter continued. "The target is selected, but in addition, I'm also talking about a patient who is obsessive, precise and efficient. Before there even was a target, he had elegantly contrived methods of assassination for some potential unknown malevolent creature. He is, I can only tell you this much, for reasons I prefer not to discuss, absorbed with death and homicide. He would like nothing better than to be a political assassin. Do not press me on this point. I do not wish to discuss why. He is not a fool or an unkind person. He would have liked to have been a young German at the time of the rise of Hitler; a soldier in the ranks of the grandiose Napoleon. I know it sounds crazy but you must believe me, he is not crazy. The specifics which I cannot offer you lend a certain degree of logic, if not reasonableness, to his position. But to answer your question, he has worked it out elaborately: details of assassination plots—most of which seem farfetched to my amateur ears. As I said, if I had thought that he was really about to execute someone I think I would intercede."

"You *think* you would intercede?" Skip asked with a note of sharpness. "You say you think you would intercede!"

"Well, no, of course I didn't mean that. I *would* intercede. I am pretty sure. I am sure I would intercede."

"Jesus, Peter, that hardly sounds convincing."

"Well, I suppose my hesitation is because the person who is currently targeted would be no great loss to humanity."

"I can't believe I hear you correctly," said Skip. "You, who are almost priggish about proprieties, who started this whole conversation with such an esoteric bullshit set of generalizations I couldn't even understand what the hell you were talking about. You, who are almost pompously moral about issues which would strike other people as precious. You're telling me that you are prepared to say who should die and who should not. Listen to yourself, man. You're talking about being an accomplice to murder! If someone is supposed to die the laws of the land take care of that, or, if one is religious, which neither one of us is, or at least never used to be—I suppose the next thing I'll hear is that you've converted to Catholicism—if one is religious, one assumes these things are in the hands of God, and that the evil man will suffer eventually; or if he does not, it is God's will that he does not, for inscrutable reasons that we mortals must respect.

"The absolute hubris of your last remark astounds me. It is so atypical. What in God's name does it mean that someone 'deserves' to die? And since when have you set yourself up as judge in these matters?"

"I didn't mean that," said Peter.

"You damn well did mean it," Skip interrupted. "Who are you telling you didn't mean it? You're the psychoanalyst, not me. We both know that you meant it, and I don't mind telling you that I'm shaken by the recognition that you meant it."

The two men stared at each other in a moment of silence and Peter noticed with astonishment that Skip had drained his glass of wine. He beckoned the waiter over and asked for a second. This small gesture unsettled Peter more than anything that had been said during the course of the past half hour. He knew the enormous struggle with alcohol that Skip had had as a young man and he knew how rigid his discipline had been over the past thirty years. He did not want to be the instrument of even more harm. Peter sighed and said:

"Okay, let's both calm down. I know for a fact that the boy *cannot*—I give you my assurance—cannot act now. I am wondering what sort of steps should be taken if in the future I arrive at a point where there is even a reasonable doubt about the feasibility of an assassination. Whom should I call? Who could institute the steps to abort the plan, and still do a minimal amount of harm to my patient? I do not want him hurt. Life has hurt him enough. He's had more than his share. I do not want him hurt, Skip."

"Before I answer that question," said Skip, "I want to understand precisely what you said. You are saying that now there is literally no chance, I repeat, *no* chance that anything can happen."

"I swear on it. By all that's holy," said Peter.

"Well," said Skip, the tension finally breaking between the two, "I'm relieved to find you swearing on anything these days."

They both laughed, pleased that the incipient argument had been avoided.

"Then, if I understand you correctly, there is absolutely no danger at the present time and we are really talking about a theoretical situation. In that case I would suggest you contact the FBI and notify them of the name of the individual, the person threatened, and the specific conditions which you refuse to describe to me, but which lead you to be convinced that it is not a serious threat. I say this because that is the professional advice I ought to offer you, and you would be acquitted then from any responsibility under law for what might happen. But I know you, buddy. And I know you will not do it. Instead, I ask you to do this. Call me when you sense any change from impossibility to remote possibility. Do you understand what I'm saying to you, Peter? I do not want you to wait even to a point of probability. I want you to call me when you sense there is even a *remote* possibility of executing the plan, and I want you then to level with me. Will you do that?"

"I think I will," said Peter.

"You think you will," said Skip. "We're back to that!"

"Oh, for God's sake," said Peter, "it won't come to that."

"It *will* come to that! I know you. You would not have come to me unless you sense that it will come to that."

"You may know me," continued Peter, "but you don't know the boy. It may come to that but I don't think it will. At any rate, certainly, when the time comes, I would think I would call you. But hell, why you? What do you do, Skip?"

"That's the question you're not supposed to ask," said Skip. "You are losing your manners. Forget about what I do. Just call me."

Chapter XV

February—five months before the convention

> Rumor has it that Roger Hilton has been
> offered a major position with UNESCO,
> but has quietly refused, adamant in his
> determination to avoid involvement with
> anything remotely suggestive of the political. (PERSPECTIVE—James Saperstein)

Lincoln McAllister was sitting at his large Georgian mahogany desk in the Fifth Avenue triplex that was considered his New York "home." Alison and the children were in the McLean home, where they stayed during the course of the school year. Often, she would join him on weekends in New York, and for that purpose they kept a small staff to maintain the apartment even in the winter months. He was alone, then, in the house except for the housekeeper and maid. It was as private as it was likely to get now that the campaign for the nomination was in full swing. He was shuffling papers distractedly, looking at the large clock, minute after minute, registering the mounting tension within him. He had not seen Jim Doyle—seen in the sense of having spent private time with him—since McAllister resigned from the Hilton administration in its second year. They had, of course, bumped into each other at political and social events, but never a private meeting, or a truly private conversation.

Lincoln McAllister would have been a logical candidate for political service in any administration that coincided with his coming of age. When beckoned by Jim Doyle he was twenty-eight years old. He had the grace, the fortune, the social standing which were so desperately needed in the Hilton administration. Doyle had known McAllister briefly at Harvard. Doyle was five years older but had started college a year late, so that he was a junior when McAllister—who had naturally started early—was a freshman. Doyle, a Boston Irishman from a poor family, had worked his way into the Harvard community, and in four years had learned the lace curtain manners and the white shoe style that belied the fact that he was a bartender's son. He was the managing editor of the Harvard *Crimson* when McAllister, against all the rules of background, chose to work for the *Crimson* rather than the *Lampoon,* where boys of his breeding were expected to pursue what literary skills they might have. Doyle was a natural newspaperman and McAllister was not. Yet Doyle respected his perseverance, his hard work and his dedication to a newspaper that was always taken as seriously by its staff as the New York *Times* is by its.

Lincoln was always confused as to why Jim Doyle spent so much time with him and was so kind to him. They played a great deal of squash together, both being superbly fit and fine athletes. And, in time, McAllister began to see Doyle as his mentor—and indeed he was. McAllister rose at the *Crimson* disproportionate to his true abilities. While much of that success was due to the enormous energy he devoted, it was apparent to everybody that he was a favorite of Jim Doyle.

It did not surprise Lincoln McAllister when, a few years later, he learned that Doyle had left the New York *Times* to join Roger Hilton. In many ways McAllister would have been a more logical candidate for the party than Doyle. Doyle was a straight investigative reporter with no particularly strong political leanings. He had, in addition, come from a traditional Irish Catholic Democratic background in Boston. People at the *Times* were therefore surprised when Hilton selected him as his Press Secretary. Hilton liked physically attractive young men around him and Doyle fit that bill in all other ways as well. In addition, it was known that Hilton was impressed with the work Doyle had done for Robert Kennedy when he was Senator from New York. Hilton had a fixation on the Kennedys, and Doyle, somehow or other, seemed a link to them. No one, however, in those days could have predicted the intensity of the relationship that developed between the two men or the fact that when Hilton left in disgrace, Jim Doyle, who had been untainted by The Scandal, would, of all the people around him, be the only one to join Hilton in the retreat to his Elba.

McAllister was roused from his thoughts by a gentle tapping on the door.

"Come in," he said.

"Mr. Doyle is here, sir," said the housekeeper.

"Show him in, Myrtle. We'll be meeting in this room; and then please hold all calls and leave us undisturbed. I'll make Mr. Doyle a drink myself."

"Yes, sir," she said, quietly leaving. She returned in a few moments, ushered Jim Doyle into the room and closed the door behind him.

McAllister was not prepared for his reaction. He was startled to see how much Doyle had aged in the last three or four years. That handsome, tanned, lean Irish face seemed to have lost all its underlying support structure.

While still good-looking, there was now a soft, jowly quality. Is that what time does, or is it drink? McAllister wondered as he unconsciously and concernedly ran his hand across his own jawline.

McAllister was also surprised at the spontaneous surge of good feeling he experienced on seeing his old friend, and the joyous smile that accompanied it was far different from the polite, courteous smile that he affected with strangers. Despite all that had happened, he still was fond of Doyle, and genuinely pleased to see him—although the curiosity about his mission persisted.

"Jim, come on in. Let me get you a drink."

"A Scotch would be fine," said Doyle as he settled into one of the two large leather chairs separated by an oversized coffee table.

McAllister had crossed to behind the desk, pushed aside some sliding doors to the built-in cabinets and revealed a fully equipped bar with refrigerator, sink and rows of liquor.

"I've got even better, I've got some Irish," said McAllister as he poured it straight into a double old-fashioned glass. He remembered that Doyle took his liquor neat.

As old friends invariably will, they began with talk of early golden days and their warm friendship in that still untainted period before the Hilton administration. Yet the perceptible tension in both men took the edge off the conversation and finally Jim Doyle said,

"Link, some other time I'd like to meet with you, and talk, and be friends, but I'm not here as Jim Doyle. I'm a messenger and I hate the role, particularly with you, so maybe I can get on with it and then we can clear the air and just be 'good old boys.'"

"You're here for *him* then," Link said, a note of distaste entering his voice despite himself. "I suspected as much. God, Jim, how could you have done it? What keeps you with him? How could you throw away your career, your life, with that man? Nobody understands."

Doyle interrupted. "And nobody will. Link, it's too complicated. Then, I'm not sure I understand. I can't go into it, and I don't want to, particularly with you.

I'll always love you"—he paused for a moment noticing Link's slight wince at the "excessiveness" of the spontaneous word—"like the young brother I never had," he continued, the pause being almost imperceptible.

McAllister had always been somewhat put off by the effusiveness of Jim Doyle's language. He loved the almost musical flow of words but he was never sure how much was Irish blarney and how much true feelings. The capacity to use words like "darling," "love of my life," jarred two hundred years of establishment WASP and North Shore reserve in Link. Doyle, knowing this, always softened the effect by affecting a slight Irish brogue during such times.

"Shall we get on with it then, darlin?" asked Jim.

"Yes, you idiot, let's get on with it," Link answered, laughing, the tension now somewhat relieved.

"Link, you must know that Red Herring was not RH's idea. I know you were not at the meeting. Neither was I—but certainly Kate briefed you. It was done without his insistence, indeed, without even the courtesy of his permission. He is, in this case, purely an instrument of your future. It was Horace Mudd's idea from beginning to end. And Horace Mudd doesn't give a damn about anything since his wife died except virtue, the United States and The Establishment. This must not then be viewed as something RH is doing to you. It is something that's being done *to* him, *for* you."

"Poor man," Link said sarcastically. "It must be agonies to be sanctified publicly, in your own time, while you're still alive. Particularly," he continued with disgust, "for so self-effacing and modest a man as Roger Hilton."

"I don't deny he's benefiting from it. I won't even deny to you that he loves it; that he's lapping it up. But it was not his idea, Link, and it is you who will benefit."

"Well, obviously, I'm going along," Link answered. "So what's the problem?"

"The problem is that you're *not* going along," Jim said somewhat sharply. "And your not going along is becoming increasingly apparent to Hilton, and shortly will be apparent to the public at large. What has been up to now a personal embarrassment will, if you continue on your current course, become a public humiliation and could in the long run defeat Red Herring. And you, Link, would be through. And I mean really through. Don't kid yourself. Your entire political future is at risk. You're playing with the big boys now. And it's a rough game. Mudd, Baker and that crowd support, embrace and revere you only as an instrument of the party and The Establishment. If you betray that trust—you're nobody. You're dead!"

"Why do you always use such flamboyant language? It always did annoy me. 'Betray.' Hell!"

"I'm sorry, Link. The last thing I want to do is anger you. I come on a mission I did not want to make. I dreaded it. I know your hatred for RH. I did not want to contaminate our relationship. We were friends once, Link. We are friends, aren't we, Link?"

"Of course," said Link, somewhat embarrassed, and without much conviction.

"All I'm asking then..." He corrected himself: "All RH is asking, is that you make some token gesture, some public statement that shows your approval, your acceptance of him."

"Accept that *shit?*"

"Link, don't make my job harder."

"I'm sorry," said McAllister. "Look, you're not saying any more to me than Kate has been for the last three weeks. And yesterday I dodged a call from Hugh Baker—always a dangerous and foolish thing to do—because I knew what he was going to say. I'm sorry, Jim, I shouldn't be putting you through this, but I cannot publicly endorse that man! There's a distinction between active endorsement, and allowing him to be restored to good public faith without interfering. I will do that. In that sense I will be a passive accomplice to the act. Morally, I suspect it's no different. It may be a form of hypocrisy, but that's as much as I can endure. I will not get up in a press conference or on public television and tell the world that Roger Hilton is a maligned, much suffering victim of a political conspiracy."

"I'm afraid, Link, that is precisely what you're going to have to do."

"What in hell do you mean, *have* to do?" demanded McAllister.

"I'm sorry, I didn't mean that. It was simply a figure of speech. I meant that's precisely what you *ought* to do, and presume that eventually you will come to do. My God, you've gotten tendentious as you've gotten older. You kept your young looks, but you've developed a temper. I think I like it."

"And you, Jim, seem to have an unlimited supply of blarney; and you know I've always liked that. But, Jim, you know I can't. Call it stubborn, call it a fault of character, I am simply too rigid. It is too much against the grain. I can bend a great deal. But I would gag on the words. I simply cannot."

There was a pause as the two men avoided looking directly at each other, and then Doyle continued, "I don't want you to get angry, Link, but you've got to understand. I'm begging you to do this. It means more to me than you realize. I'm begging you to say right now, 'I'll do this for you, Jim,' or for my own career or for Kate or for Alison or for the country. I'm begging you, Link, as much as if I were on my hands and knees to you. Just say you'll make some gesture. After all, that's all he's asking now."

"Did you say now? What does that mean, *now?* He's talked about more! That son of a bitch has a plan, doesn't he? He's going to ask for more later on. He's already plotting how to use the fake respectability that's now being tailored for him. That fucking respectability is just the camel's nose in the tent. That son of a bitch wants more, doesn't he?"

Doyle was upset with himself for the use of the word which betrayed conversations he had desperately not wanted to introduce at this point. Link was too smart, and knew him too well for a total denial at this point. His heart was pounding. He felt himself trapped in a direction which terrified him.

"I don't *know* whether he'll want more," he lied. "It's not inconceivable that after the election he might ask for an ambassadorship to some remote place."

"He might ask!" exploded McAllister.

"I didn't say he would," Jim said. "He might, and

then you're free to refuse. But why should you? It would get him out of the country. For God's sake, you're twenty-five years younger than he is. The man will die. Don't press this thing. Your strong suit was always your rationality, your temperate sensibility. What's happening to you?"

"I won't give that son of a bitch the time of day now. And you can tell him that for me. And that's all I want to hear about it," warned McAllister.

Doyle then seemed to collapse into himself. And McAllister noticed with concern, He does seem old. I wonder if he's sick. Something is wrong.

"So it comes to this," Doyle said. "Sweet Jesus, it comes to this." He closed his eyes.

"Jim, what's wrong?" Link said with deep concern. "Are you all right?"

Doyle started to talk but couldn't get words out. The tears were coming from his eyes. A choked sound, like a muffled sob, escaped from his mouth.

McAllister was in a near panic. He couldn't tolerate tears, even from his wife, and this kind of show of emotion from a man was almost unbearable.

"Jim, for God's sake," he continued, "what's the matter? Control yourself, Jim."

He noticed that Doyle's right hand had been gripping the side of the heavy armchair with such intensity that it had blanched white. He now lifted that hand off the chair, wiped his eyes with the back of the hand and said, "I'm sorry, Link. I'm so sorry. If I had the balls, I would have cut my throat before I came here today."

"Jesus, Jim, there's nothing to be so sorry about. You asked; I refused."

"Oh, Link, you always were so direct, so simple. If only there were a little deviousness in you, you could have been a great man. Not that you won't be a good man and a decent President. But if only you had some Irish cunning, some Jewish 'shechel,' you could have been a truly great man. It's not what I have said that bothers me. It's what I'm about to say. Forgive me, Link," he continued, "but you do remember that night at the White House pool?"

With this last statement Doyle turned his head

away, averting his gaze from McAllister's steady inquisitive stare. McAllister's body tensed noticeably. He looked straight ahead, blinked his eyes a few times and gave a slight, almost imperceptible sideways shake of his head. His eyelids began to blink rapidly and compulsively as if in a spasm or twitch. But he didn't move from his rigid posture in the chair and didn't say a word. He was like a man in an hypnoid state, not sure whether he was awake or asleep. Then with an almost uncontrollable steady sideways shaking of his head—as though with that motion he could avoid that which was emerging—he tried to deny what he heard. He hoped to convince himself that if he roused himself, if he could only command his body, he would find that which transpired was the ephemeral residue of an already fading dream.

There had been many nights at the White House pool, but to Lincoln McAllister, "that night at the White House pool" could only mean one. It was shortly after Roger Hilton's State of the Union message, the high point of his career. McAllister had worked on the first draft and Jim Doyle had completed and shaped it. It was an atypical Hilton speech, with no vitriol and no snideness. With things going his way, the President had allowed himself the highest and noblest of tones. Link had been particularly proud of the fact that four paragraphs dealing with aspirations for the future—which he had written with trepidation and the assumption that they would be excised because of a visionary and romantic quality about them—had come back from Doyle without a mark on them and with the word "beautiful" inscribed on the border. He had felt like a teen-age boy who had been given an A by a teacher. In terms of political writing Jim Doyle was his hero and his ideal and his master.

When the President, then, had incorporated the paragraphs into his final presentation and the speech was complimented even by the usually hostile press, there had been a sense of euphoria and elation in the White House. The President had insisted that Doyle and McAllister have a quiet dinner with him and then, in his not-to-be-refused manner, had suggested they go for a midnight dip in the pool. The President always insisted they go skinny-dipping and McAllister always endured this with a certain degree of reserve and distaste—a residual modesty he retained from his New England forebears.

The President enjoyed the pool and they played a modified version of water polo, closer to a free-for-all. It was every man for himself with a lot of roughhousing and body contacts. When there were larger groups, they would divide into teams, but with just the three of them, the body contact seemed somewhat suggestive, even threatening in a peculiar way. The traditional deference with which Doyle treated the President disappeared in the pool and a familiarity, almost an affectionate adolescent rapport replaced it. At these times McAllister felt like an intruder, as though witnessing some private ritual. The other two seemed ready to receive him if he wished to join the distinctly changed set of relationships, but equally ready to allow him to remain the detached observer. This was only the second time that he had been involved in so private a scene, although he had been part of the larger pool parties of the White House staff, and like the first time, he remembered thinking: Only now does Hilton seem a real human being. The "as if" quality seemed erased and a kind of gauche, rambunctious, but pathetically likable boy seemed to appear.

It was also at this time that Lincoln became concerned about the rumors of homosexuality between Doyle and the President that occasionally drifted in the inner circles. Although he quickly brushed these thoughts aside, nonetheless, he was aware that frequently during the course of the games the President had erections and this disturbed him. At the same time, he himself was aware of the sensual and sexual quality of sport and hard play.

He remembered every detail of that game even today with such vividness, with such detail—the kinds of things that are meant to be forgotten—but to this day he could describe each point and somehow, and somewhere, he was aware that the acuteness of that memory was a screen to cover the cloudiness and confusion of that which followed. It was as if by compensation the more he remembered about the activities at the pool, the less he had to remember about the ensuing scene in the exercise room.

Somewhere during the game he had wrenched his shoulder, and complained about it when the President, Doyle and he were in the sauna. These evenings usually ended with Doyle giving the President a massage, the President often falling asleep on the table. But Hilton excused himself this night, saying he was tired, and suggested—in that way that men in authority have where suggestion and order become confused—that Doyle massage the kink out of Link's shoulder. They had had a stiff drink, a Scotch, neat, and McAllister, unused to the drink and the heat of the sauna, was by that time himself dizzy and cloudy.

Is that a rationalization? McAllister wondered. Was it true? Could he really not remember the details? Did he want to?

He had gone into the room. He remembered sitting on the table and a soothing feeling of Jim Doyle's strong fingers manipulating his upper back, his shoulder and arms. Then Doyle gently guided his shoulders down to the table. The table was lit almost like an operating table, or was it like a pool table, or was there a difference? He remembered the light bothering his eyes and he closed them as Doyle gently laid a towel across them.

Doyle kept telling him he was tense, and to relax, and joked with him, saying it was his Puritan background; that sensual pleasure was sensual pleasure, and with his eyes closed he wouldn't know if it were the hands of a man or woman; to "just enjoy himself." Doyle was dipping his hands into the emollient creams, and gently rubbing them across McAllister's shoulders at first, and now his upper torso.

The conversation somehow or other got onto masturbation and he remembered being shocked as Doyle revealed to him that he often masturbated Hilton to ejaculation, saying it was an essential "part of a complete massage," calling it less a sexual act than a relaxant, a soporific.

He remembered vague talk of homosexuality, and

Doyle remarking on the arbitrariness of language. "What is and what is not homosexual"—and much elliptical talk of neutral sexual pleasures and the like. Doyle denied the President was a homosexual. Masturbation was simply a means of release for a man who was himself not very libidinous, a man uncomfortable with women, and ill at ease with sensuality. It was fairly common knowledge among the staff that the Hiltons had a celibate marriage, for at least the period they had been in the White House. The President had no lovers; that would have been readily detectable.

Vaguely, McAllister remembered thinking: Of course, it is not the President, it is Doyle who is the homosexual. But by this time he was half asleep and confused as to what was reality and what dream. His normal repulsion to physical contact with a man had faded with the slippage of consciousness, and the fingers softly gliding across his flesh brought a complete relaxation and an abandonment of resistance to the very real sensual pleasure. When the fingers, now greased with an emollient cream, began to massage his legs and thighs, he suddenly experienced a surge of warmth suffusing his groin and he began to be aware of an emerging erection. He struggled to get up. Yet all the time Doyle continued the gentle, almost lyrical talk, like a lullaby with undistinguishable words, while gently, but firmly, pinning him to the table with his forearm. McAllister began to resist clumsily and ineffectually. But did he resist or was he not really enjoying it? In the end he ceased struggling, succumbing to the total sensual pleasure of the agile fingers, and as the hands moved across his scrotum and onto the shaft of his organ, he remembered the extreme intensity of his erection, and finally in some time-suspended state, an ejaculation that seemed explosive, and totally releasing. To this day he was not aware of whether Doyle had brought him to climax by mouth or had simply used his moist, slippery fingers.

Almost instantly he had fallen asleep, or passed out from the whiskey, or perhaps had forced himself to unconsciousness to block the awareness of just what had happened. He was not sure. All he knew was that when he next opened his eyes Doyle was standing there, dressed, gently talking to him, urging him awake. By that time, whether drunk or feigning drunkenness, the distinction had no relevance. Doyle helped him to dress, unself-consciously joking and teasing. He recalled his own embarrassment at seeing Doyle, fully dressed, kneeling beside the massage table, putting on his shoes and socks like a mother with a child. Doyle drove him home as though nothing had happened, undressed him and put him to bed.

Neither of them had ever mentioned this event again. Nor had there been any further physical contact, or any change in either familiarity or manner between the two men. It was as though to have altered the relationship in any manner would be to acknowledge the reality of the event, and McAllister preferred to pretend it had never happened. Doyle, an unadjusted, guilt-ridden homosexual, had built his life of discipline and humiliation, of frustration and pent-up passions. He had learned to accept his sexual pleasures when and where they were available, and to bear with dignity whatever responses and consequences issued forth.

No mention of that had been made until this day. And McAllister, shaken, and in a cold sweat, could not believe that Doyle after all these years, would be bringing this up, and at this time.

"What do you want, Doyle?" McAllister said through clenched teeth, barely controlling the mounting anger and bewilderment showing on his face. "What in hell do you want?"

"For God's sake, Link, I don't want anything. It's the President. He wants you to be decent to him. He wants very little from you. He simply wants an acknowledgment of support, some statement of compassion or sympathy. That's all he wants. I swear it. That's all he wants."

"I don't give a shit what he wants," said McAllister. "I'm not talking to the President. I'm talking to you. I asked you what you want?"

"Link, don't do this to me. I'm the President's man. He's talking through me."

"What do you want, goddamn you! I asked what you want."

"You've got it wrong, Link. I've *got* to go along. Jesus, Link, don't you understand? *You've* got to go along. Everybody else is. Why are you so stubborn?"

"I've got to go along?"

"Link, there are pictures. There are movies."

McAllister was stunned and didn't say anything for a moment. At first he wasn't quite sure what Doyle was talking about. What did he mean, pictures—movies? And, then, slowly, the horrible realization.

"You dirty, cheap fag, you! You set me up. You both set me up."

"On my mother's life, Link," Doyle said, tears breaking into his eyes again. "On my mother's life, Link, you cannot believe that. I didn't know. None of us knew."

"Did you know of the tapes?"

"I swear to God I knew nothing. The whole goddamn White House was bugged. There were only three people who knew anything about the tapes and I wasn't one of them. I thought I knew everything about him. Everyone else assumed I knew everything about him. I didn't know about this.

"He is smart. Certain information he shared with some intimates, others were best left to technicians. Nobody but he and the technicians knew about the tapes, or about the movies. He was never a man who opened up to anyone. He still doesn't. You once asked me if he was a homosexual. He's not. He's nothing. He's a neuter, a person who relates to no one. Anyway, I'm the homosexual. I'm the closet queen. And in a peculiar way I'm bound to him. I love him. I'm disgusted by him, but I like serving him. I even, God help me, like being humiliated by him. Had I been born twenty years later, when homosexuality was more acceptable, maybe I would have had a healthier outlet. I could have had lovers. But it's not my style. I could never go public. I get furtive pleasures and small gratifications. For the most part, it's just fantasy and masturbation. There was a sexuality to my serving the President. His power, his coldness excited me. He knew it. He used it. He still does. Don't ask me about it. It's sick."

"I would do almost anything for the President, Link; but not this. I would never do this to you. You're the younger brother I never had. Don't you see that I'm not lying? You're the lover I always wanted. I would never hurt you. It was I, as well as you, who was set up."

Doyle continued to ramble, half crying, half begging. McAllister was no longer listening. A sick, faint nausea had swept from the pit of his stomach and now seemed to envelop his entire body. He no longer even thought of himself and his potential exposure. He could not bear seeing Doyle so emasculated, so reduced. Had he been another man, he might have put his arm around him and comforted him. Instead he simply said,

"It's all right, Jim. I don't want to talk about it any more. I believe you. It's all right."

Doyle pulled himself together.

"What are you going to do?"

McAllister said, resignedly, but with a certain resolution in his tone, "You're going to go back and tell him you did your job. And I..." There was a pause. "I will have to think about it."

"He'll use it, Link. He'll use it if he has to."

"I know he will, Jim."

"Don't be so goddamn moralistic and unbending; give him some small token. That's all he wants. Don't throw away a career for some stiff pride."

"I'll think about it, Jim. Small gestures have ways of getting expanded. I don't trust that bastard. He'll want more."

"Jesus, Link, how much more can he want? He's an old man. All he wants is a shred of respectability returned to him."

"He doesn't deserve it. Jim, get yourself home."

With that statement McAllister extended his hand to shake that of his former friend. It was meant as a gesture of conciliation and was accepted as such. Doyle turned around and let himself out the door.

McAllister walked to the bathroom and vomited into the toilet. Then he doused his head under the cold water, wiped himself dry with a linen towel—and dialed Kate Parr.

Chapter XVI

February—that night

Kate Parr had gone to bed early. Laura was out of town directing a play at the Guthrie Theater. She missed her. The two women did not live together, but they tended to share most nights, and when they did it was usually in Kate's apartment. Laura's place was not much more than a pied-à-terre. She traveled a great deal, and maintained an old house in Vermont, left to her by her father, that she thought of as home.

Kate had been exhausted by the increasing pressure as the nomination drew closer. The campaign, which should have been—which, indeed, had been—greased to a point of perfect functioning, was now a nightmare of friction. And all because of an unpredictable intransigence on the part of Lincoln McAllister. From all sides the pressure funneled through her. Almost daily, the calls now came asking for "some small gesture" that could be seen as a public acknowledgment by Lincoln McAllister of the new, more respectable position of Roger Hilton.

Normally, she worked closely with Link through the evening, rarely getting home before midnight. He had told her this afternoon that she should take the evening off; that he had an important private meeting. While she relished the thought of a quiet, unharried evening alone, she was surprised and somewhat hurt by the uncharacteristic vagueness of his allusion. Usually, he would have told her the what, when and where. Tonight it was simply an "appointment." Nonetheless, she was grateful enough for the unexpected reprieve from the pressures and tensions, that she thought no more of it.

Hundreds of neglected items of everyday routine

seemed scattered across her apartment as they were scattered through her life. She was amazed how little time she had to devote to the simple nuts and bolts of her own personal life. Every energy bent to the service of Lincoln McAllister. One of these days, she thought, she was going to find herself without charge accounts, electricity or even a telephone. That, come to think of it, could be a blessing.

She had used the evening partially getting her desk in order and then, with total exhaustion, had taken a bath and gone to bed around ten o'clock. When the phone rang she was in that deep state of unconsciousness that characterizes the first few hours of sleep. She was disoriented, vaguely remembering the tail end of some disturbing dream. The phone ringing had still not penetrated total consciousness, and she automatically reached over to embrace Laura. At that point she heard the phone again, coincident with the awareness that Laura was not there.

My God, she thought, what time is it? Who is ringing? What is it? Panic seized her and she began to feel a rise of that unknown terror that emerges so readily in that twilight state between waking and sleeping. Something has happened to Laura, she thought. Who would be calling at this hour? And as she reached for the phone, she noticed, to her surprise, that it was only just midnight.

It was Link, but his voice sounded shrill, high-pitched and hesitant. He had only to say, "Kate, I need you," when she responded, "I'll be there in ten minutes," and hung up.

That was the entire conversation and yet she was alerted: something awful had happened. She knew it as surely as if the details had been explicated in a half-hour speech. She didn't bother to dress, simply putting on a sweater, slacks, and slipping into the Nikes that were tucked under her bed, waiting for her morning run. How the hell am I going to get there? I'll walk, she thought with anxiety. She was afraid to walk at night even though the fifteen blocks from her apartment on Seventy-second and Second Avenue to his on Sixty-third and Fifth was through the safest and most elegant sections of New York. She hated to admit her fear. It made her recognize the special vulnerability that still existed in being a woman.

She started to leave when she remembered her brief case, and without knowing what was going on, thought it might be best to bring it. At the same time she quickly called the doorman, asking him to see if he could hail a cab. She gathered the current notes lying on her desk that she had not yet shown Link: the outline of a speech he was to give in three weeks, some letters that were to go out under his name, and a brief sketch she had written formulating his acceptance speech at the nomination. All were shoved quickly into the brief case. Although she sensed they would be unnecessary, they somehow reassured her that this would be simply another working meeting. She needed every bit of reassurance now. She emerged from the elevator and ran down the short corridor to the front entrance of the building. She was delighted and relieved to find a cab waiting for her.

Link opened the door for her himself. She immediately noticed a slight tremor in his hands. She had seen this before at moments of great tension. It was, she presumed, the strain of holding in emotions that were normally readily expressed by other people. She always visualized his holding back, his great reserve, as though it were an actual muscular act, like keeping a door closed against pressure from the other side.

"I'm sorry, Kate. I'm so sorry. You have so few evenings. I shouldn't impose."

He seemed awkward, standing in the doorway, and she wasn't sure how she would get by, to enter the room. This total uncharacteristic gracelessness was more disturbing than anything he might have said. The moment of standing in the open doorway seemed interminable. Finally, she gently pressed him aside as she reached behind and closed the door herself. Yet he continued to stand there, muttering in the same slowed-down speech that she had detected on the phone, this inane cliché—"I'm so sorry to have imposed on your free evening."

"Link, there are no free evenings for me where you're

concerned. There never will be. Link, don't be polite. Remember, it's Kate."

She couldn't bear to see him in such distress. It was so atypical. She wanted to put her arms around him; to hug him; to rock him gently. She had done as much for Laura, and indeed Laura for her, and she knew the comfort of a simple physical embrace. My God, she had done it for other men for whom she cared not one portion of the amount she cared for Link. And yet, with him, the only man besides her father she had ever loved, she could not. She loved him in an inexplicable way as she loved no one else, not even Laura. But she could not bring him into her arms, where he belonged, for he could not tolerate it. He would not understand, and it would only bring pain rather than comfort; anxiety rather than security. Instead, she took his hand and brought it to her cheek. It was a gesture that he had used with her on occasions of particular closeness. She felt that the borrowing of it now, would be unthreatening and acceptable. To her surprise and delight, rather than quickly withdrawing his hand, he pressed it against her cheek for a moment. It seemed to calm him. She guided him to the tufted leather chair, where he traditionally relaxed, and she sat on the ottoman at his feet. He immediately began to talk.

At first he started theoretically, and in the most general terms. He talked about blackmail, and capitulation; honor and ruin. The speech was rambling, and apocalyptic. She could not understand to what he was alluding, but she recognized that his need for catharsis was greater than her need for understanding and she allowed him this atypical rush of words.

Eventually, he collected himself and methodically recapitulated the entire conversation with Jim Doyle; sparing himself nothing, leaving out no details. He did not look at her.

During the entire monologue he sat slouched forward in his armchair, head bent down and forward, staring intently at his own hands clenched together in front of him, like a schoolboy's.

"It's all over, Kate. It's all over. I don't know what I'll do; but I know it's all over."

Kate could not stand seeing him hunched that way in the posture of defeat. She had no idea what to do to restore his confidence, to revive his usual composure. That strong, external control, which she had resented so often in the past, was urgently needed now. She realized the defensive purposes of that armor, and she knew no way to help him regird so that he could be prepared to face with her the practical problems. He seemed so impotent, so helpless, and she could not bear this strange and alien Lincoln McAllister sitting opposite her.

For a moment she wondered if the direct way might not be the simplest; how better to restore a man's sense of his own manhood than by going to bed with him? God knows she had wanted it often enough, and, in a peculiar way, his very vulnerability made him more accessible and appealing. She felt a surge of sexual passion and now it was she who desperately wanted to make love to him, independent of his needs. She started to make a gesture towards him but then instinctively recognized that it would be a horrible mistake. She sensed he would acquiesce—but it would be wrong. Their love—and it was a form of love—was the romantic love of the days of chivalry. It was the very unrequited nature of that adoration, like that of a twelfth-century knight and his lady, that sustained it through a lifetime. So she resisted her impulse. Instead, she simply took his clenched hands in her hands and gently kissed them. He looked up for the first time.

She rose then, mixed herself a drink and sat in a chair across from his. "We must get down to work, Link. We don't have much time. We have to decide how to handle this."

The very businesslike nature of the pose and language she adopted had a therapeutic effect. He smiled. And they began a discussion of the rational alternatives.

"In a sense, Link, this alters nothing. I have begged you—we all have begged you—to make that small gesture required of you."

"I will not respond to blackmail."

"This is not a response to blackmail. My God, Link, how many times did I beg you to do what Jim Doyle was asking you to do tonight, without any knowledge of the film? Was my asking you then a form of blackmail or was it simply common sense? For the moment, forget the incident tonight. There were good reasons why you should have acquiesced before. I am not talking about the blackmail. We are right back to where we were before Jim Doyle made his ugly visit. You will make some small gesture, not because you are being blackmailed, but because you are the smart politician I know you are; because the gesture will not damage you; and because sophisticated and wise men who have your interest at heart have insisted that you make the gesture."

"And what will be the next gesture after the first, and the next after that, and the next—and when will it cease being a gesture and become a substantive move? And when will it cease being a request, but a demand? And when will I be serving him, rather than he serving me?"

"That will not happen, Link. I promise you that will not happen."

"For God's sake, Kate, Hilton's got these films! You don't want to hear, any more than I want to remember. He's got that fucking film. He would use it even if he didn't have to. He's the kind of man who enjoys doing things like that! You simply aren't listening to me."

"I do not want to talk about the film. Not tonight. It's too soon to think clearly about that. I simply want to impress on you that sooner or later you are going to have to make an accommodation. The film we can forget about for now. Think about the political reasons for making the accommodation, and that will buy us time. Forget the goddamn film."

"Forget the film," he said incredulously. "I don't believe you. Forget the goddamn Lincoln McAllister-as-fag film."

"Link, I promise you. That film will never be used. It will be destroyed. I will see Hugh Baker tomorrow morning. He will find a way. I promise you, he will never allow that film to be used."

"How can you be sure?"

"I know Hugh Baker. I can be sure. Now, Link, will you promise to make an accommodation?"

"I don't know," he said, but obviously calmed. "I don't know what I will do. I promise you I will think about it."

She smiled. His stubbornness was a sign of the reorganization of his defenses. She had done her job. The old Lincoln McAllister was sitting opposite her; tense, but collected. It was now up to her, she realized. She had work to do. My God, she had work to do! She wondered if it was too late to call Baker tonight.

Chapter XVII

March—four months before the convention

> Distinguished among the visitors to the bedside of Elizabeth Hilton, was Katherine Parr, Executive Assistant to Lincoln McAllister. Observers were quick to notice that this represents, if only indirectly, the first rapprochement between Lincoln McAllister and Roger Hilton since Hilton's return to public life. (CBS News)

Herbert Shaffer had started seeing Dr. Peter Moss some eight months after his appointment to the federal judiciary. He was a quiet, contemplative man, with a sardonic humor and enormous capacity for scholarship. He had been inexplicably offered the appointment to the bench during one of those periods of pressure for "nonpolitical" appointments to the District Court. At the time he was Professor of Constitutional Law at New York University Law School. The migraine headaches which had resisted all medical treatment became intensified with the added burdens of the public position and the anguish of a conscientious man in a difficult role. Finally, with little hope, and much trepidation about possible exposure, he sought psychoanalytic treatment. To his amazement the treatment had proved effective in eliminating the headaches which had tortured him since his days in law school. At this point he was almost thankful for them, for they had become the vehicle for his seeking treatment which had resolved a wide range of neurotic attitudes which had constricted his life without his having been even aware that he was limited. The release of emotionality, starting with the pent-up anger that had led to the migraines, quickly spread to affection, tenderness and a wider range of emotions that had been bound within him. To the outside world Herbert Shaffer was still a diffident and controlled person, but his internal life had changed and he would be forever indebted to Moss.

He walked into the office in a forward-leaning posture that always reminded Moss of Mr. Hulot. He placed his hat on the chair near the couch in his usual way and then hesitated, rather than moving directly to the couch.

"Excuse me, Doctor," he said with his usual formality. "I think, perhaps, I would like to sit up and face you today."

Moss was startled. This predictable man always followed the rules, so when he chose not to, Moss was aware that it was not for trivial reasons.

"Of course," Moss answered quickly. "Please sit down."

"Thank you," the judge responded stiffly.

The two men then sat there facing each other in a moment of silence, adjusting to this unusual break in the traditional pattern.

"I don't know where to begin," Shaffer said.

Moss remained silent.

"I'm not even sure," the judge continued, "that this has anything to do with my analysis, and I really feel it would be best left unsaid."

"Everything that occurs to you has to do with the analysis," Moss replied.

"It goes beyond that," Shaffer said. "It puts me in a conflict of interests. What I have to say, Doctor, has nothing to do with me or my personal problems, but has to do with my authority and position as a federal judge. As you are bound to secrecy in your arena, so am I in mine, and yet..." He left the sentence unfinished.

"And yet what?" Moss asked encouragingly.

The judge remained silent. He was distressed and showed his moral anguish in his inability to face his doctor.

"It's a most awkward position," the judge continued. "I really don't know what I am supposed to do. The simplest thing would be for me to walk out of this office and walk out of treatment. But my treatment is too important to me and I won't do that."

Moss shifted in his chair, leaning forward toward the judge, trying not to show the degree to which he was surprised by the last statement. It was not uncommon at all for patients to be faced with a conflict in their role between the demands of privacy and trust in their personal life and the demands for openness that the analytic procedure demanded for therapeutic effectiveness. It had always seemed clear to him—and in ways not quite explicable he had tacitly let his patients know—that to speak to an analyst was not, truly, to violate the trust of privacy. In addition, names need not be mentioned nor details explicated.

Judge Shaffer was not a man to speak in hyperboles, so Moss was particularly confused as to what could be the substance of his ambivalence.

"But surely you have faced this before. You have discussed things which judges call private, and yet you have not felt you have violated your trust."

"But never before," the judge answered, "have you been a principal."

"A principal? I don't understand."

"The confidential information that has passed my desk, Doctor, is about you."

As he said this—for the first time since beginning the hour—Judge Shaffer looked up and stared directly into the eyes of Peter Moss.

"You see, it is really a dilemma," he said, the humor of the situation beginning to mitigate his anxiety. "To tell my psychiatrist is to violate the code of my office. Unless, Doctor, you are capable of separating you from you, and even then, can I?"

Moss's silence was not the calculated analytic maneuver, but simply the tactical silence of a man bewildered. What in God's name was the man talking about; and what indeed was the moral position here; and who the hell cared? Moss thought. At that point his own anxiety was mounting as he wondered what in the world could be his involvement with the federal judiciary.

"The whole thing seems so melodramatic," continued the judge. "I'm afraid I may be building this up more than is warranted, particularly since I've already acted. Well, I knew the moment I came in this office that the mere coming meant that I had already committed myself to a decision. Why I had to go through with this ritual I don't know. Perhaps it has to do with my conscience, although it still leaves us with a problem, Doctor. To get on with it then. I received a request this morning for a permit to place a tap on your telephone."

"A tap on my phone!" Moss repeated involuntarily.

"And, Doctor," the judge continued, "on the grounds of high priority and national security."

"I can't believe it," Moss responded.

"Believe it, Doctor, it is true. When I raised objections on the grounds of your being a psychiatrist and the extreme confidentiality that might be broken, it turned out that it was precisely that confidentiality they wished broken. You see, Doctor, I am assured it is not you who is the security risk, but one of your patients. The details of the case were so sketchy that I refused the demand until the name of the patient could be supplied and more specificity as to the nature of the security threat could be explicated. They were vague and evasive, so I had enough grounds for refusing the request without worrying about my own personal vulnerability in refusing. I can tell you this, though, Doctor, the orders originated from the highest levels of the Justice Department. They mean business, and if the past is any guide for the future, the failure to receive a court order is not going to stop them."

Moss listened, fascinated. But as he began to be aware of the only potential source of his problem he felt his face flush as the angry recognition broke into consciousness. He maintained his silence.

"If they are seeking, whatever they are seeking, as a fishing expedition, they are going to use a very broad net indeed. Do you understand what I am saying, Doctor? It will not simply be telephone surveillance. I do not think they would go so far as to bug your office; I think the scandals in Washington have bought us some time in that area of privacy, but one never knows. Nevertheless, I suspect your office is being watched, your patients catalogued and followed. I knew I ran the risk of exposure by coming here today. That part of the decision I had made. To hell with them. So it will be on file somewhere in the FBI or CIA that I am undergoing psychiatric treatment. For me it may mean that I will never make Circuit Court of Appeals, but there is little they can do to me now. I am happy, at least for the time being, where I am. But you ought to know. And what you do with the information is your affair. You may have other patients more vulnerable than I am. And now I think I'll return to the safety of the couch," the judge said, rising and walking quickly over to the couch.

Characteristically, the mere articulation of the problem in the analyst's office seemed to have removed the weight of the burden for him, and Judge Shaffer continued that process of free association whereby he moved quickly from the discussion of a specific problem to his personal and general problem of trust and confidence. He recalled a particularly poignant instance of having stumbled upon some secrets of his brother and rival, and being torn with both the desire to expose them to his father and guilt over the desire.

The mounting rage in Peter Moss made the continuation of the session agonizing. Again and again, he had to force himself to pick up the threads of half-heard statements of his patient and to check his own fantasies and emotions. The hour seemed an eternity and he realized with relief that Shaffer was his last patient for the day. He had a dinner meeting that night which would have to be broken. He had to get to the bottom of this and he knew with absolute assurance where the bottom lay.

Once the session was concluded, Moss closed the double doors of his office, returned quickly to his desk and dialed his home number. With exasperation he heard the busy signal, slammed down the receiver and dialed the private, unlisted number he had installed to make sure he could get through the barrier of teen-age daughters. His wife answered at once.

"Listen, Ann. I'm in a little bit of a hurry. Look in our phone book and find the private number that Skip gave us. Not his Georgetown number, but the number where he said he could be reached in emergencies. Would you get it for me, please, dear?" He waited and found himself tearing at the end of the blotter. "Damn," he said audibly, annoyed at the external signs of his distress.

"Is there anything wrong, dear?" Ann had given him the number. She felt the tension in his voice.

"No," he said, trying to muster reassurance. "It's just some information that I need about a problem. Ann, I may not be going to that meeting. I'm not sure when I'll be getting home. Don't expect me for dinner but I'll call you as soon as I know what my plans are. I've got to go now."

She was used to these quick telephone calls, often between patient-hours, and their abrupt conclusions.

Immediately he picked up the phone again and dialed the Washington number. After an interminable number of clicks the call went through and on the first ring he was relieved to hear the pickup. A woman's voice answered with the crisp neutrality of the experienced secretary, "Hugh Baker's wire."

"I'd like to speak to Mr. Baker, please."

"May I ask who is calling?"

"Just tell him a friend." Now, why did I say that? he thought. After a moment's pause he heard a familiar voice on the phone, saying,

"This is Hugh Baker."

141

"You son of a bitch. You dirty, rotten, lousy son of a bitch."

"Peter? Peter, is that you?"

"You know fucking well who it is."

"Peter, listen to me. Don't say a word. I think I know what this is all about. I don't want to talk about it on the phone. Do you understand me, Peter?"

"You bastard. I don't give a shit what you want."

"Peter, listen to me. Please. I'm taking the next shuttle. I'll be in New York in two hours. I'll meet you at your office. Be there, Peter."

"Fuck you. I'll be where I goddamn well please."

"I'm leaving right now, Peter. I'll see you at your office," he said, and he hung up the phone.

Chapter XVIII

March—four months before the convention (same day)

It had taken Baker almost an hour to make the necessary calls but he still managed to make the second section of the seven o'clock shuttle. He had arranged to meet Moss at his office rather than at home, recognizing there was still the possibility that Ann Moss might be totally unaware of what was going on. Peter's protection of the privacy of his patients had passed over from an early vigilance to an automatic stage. It was possible, therefore, that Ann did not know, and if so it was important that she should not.

During the cab ride from LaGuardia he began to sort out his emotions from the facts, and his desires from his obligations. Baker was nothing if not orderly. His personal life had always been separated from his professional life. Indeed, the covert and overt aspects of his professional life had been maintained in almost totally separate identities. Nonetheless, his primary responsibility was always cast in terms of his governmental duty. He took pride in the fact that he still pursued his scholarly career, and was respected in the academic community. Now there was a new question of conflicting roles and ambiguous loyalties. Peter Moss was an old friend, and friendship did not come easy in later life. Loyalty to friends was as much a part of his New England tradition as loyalty to country and responsibility to his job. The conflict of these loyalties was unsettling and raising his emotional level. And Baker did not ordinarily allow emotions to intrude on the rational process.

Fortunately, Moss's office—like many psychiatrists'—was in an ordinary residential apartment building, on East Eighty-ninth Street, with the typical casual doorman, and no problems of signing in or signing out. He took the elevator to the fifth floor, walked into the unlocked door to the waiting room and steeled himself for the confrontation.

The two men had been going at each other for close to two hours now and both were near a state of emotional depletion. The early calm and control had given way to anger, and now had once again returned to the calm that characterizes emotional exhaustion. Everything that needed to be said had been said twice, and then a third time only because neither of them seemed to know how to resolve the evening with their pride and their duty intact. Both men now sat silently.

"I guess I still don't understand," said Moss, "how you as my oldest friend could have treated me this way. Over all these years it was *you* who had confided in *me*—personal problems, family crises, children. I guess because of the nature of my job, it was mostly your confiding in me. And never once did I violate that trust. Jesus, Skip, neither one of us is the kind of person who violates trust. And then for you to do this! It's not just a breach of confidence and a betrayal of friendship—you could have destroyed me professionally. And it's not a trivial job I have, Hugh."

"Neither is mine," Baker replied.

"I guess you just don't understand the nature of my work."

"No, I understand fully," responded Baker, "but I don't think you understand—or want to understand—the nature of *my* work. You're still thinking of Hugh Baker, academician and scholar. Please try to understand. I think if you once grasped who I really am and what I really do, it would make more sense to you.

"I can't go into details—I won't go into details—but for God's sake, Pete, you must realize by now I'm a critical central figure in the security apparatus of this country. We haven't talked politics for a long time; since 'our war' there has been the Korean War and the Vietnam War, and those two unpopular wars seemed to make the fact of national survival seem less important. But remember those days when we were in college and the Nazis were destroying Europe? For God's sake, you must remember how eager we both were at seventeen to get involved.

"You're out of all that now. I'm not. Maybe you don't see situations recurring analogous to that. I do. Maybe I'm wrong. But certainly I'm entitled to the same responsibilities to my convictions now as then."

"All right. Maybe I don't understand. Maybe I can't afford to understand," Moss interrupted. "And maybe I just don't want to understand. But it wasn't just a breach of confidence about a patient. Jesus, Skip, you were going to destroy my professional life. Oh, that sounds stupid. Maybe you have a right to do that in the interests of 'national security.' I don't know how to explain what I mean. You were attacking not just me, or my job, but the very nature of my profession, it seems to me. And what about my patients, and the innocents who would suffer with the exposure? I don't know. I seem to be making such a poor case. What you were going to do was wrong. Damn it, I know it was wrong. It was disgusting. You just don't understand the nature of my work."

"Oh, bullshit," said Baker quietly and without anger. By this time both men were totally drained and the talk was really no longer for amplification but merely a stalling for time so that each of them could reach for an appropriate resolution to the impasse.

"It's that you don't understand or won't understand what occurred. Let's look at what happened: you come up to me, a high-ranking security officer—without your awareness, I grant that—but nonetheless, goddamn it, that's what I am," he said with rising inflection. "A high-ranking security officer. You give me a lot of mumbo jumbo about some theoretical patient with some theoretical analyst who may assassinate some theoretical major political figure and then some mealy-mouthed assurances that 'you don't think,' 'in all likelihood'—'according to your best estimations' and all that crap—'of course he will not really do it.' I know you, Peter, and I know your style, and I know you don't like to talk. And damn it, I may not be a psychoanalyst, but you don't have a monopoly on the understanding of human beings. I knew damn well how serious it was and how worried you were.

"So what would you have me do? Sit on my ass? Betray my job? Betray my country? Of course I was in a bind. I don't like betraying a friend, but you wouldn't tell me! And I was supposed to go to bed nights sleeping comfortably with your not terribly reassuring predictions that you didn't *think* it would happen. You also don't have to be a psychiatrist to know that psychological predictions of behavior are shit."

"Couldn't you trust me?" asked Moss.

"Did you trust me? You never leveled with me. You still won't. You haven't told me who, what, where, when. If you had trusted me, then I could have trusted you. You set the rules, damn it. Not me."

"I didn't set the rules. For God's sake, Skip, for the sixth time, let me repeat. The rules of confidentiality are not my rules. They're the foundation of trust on which the whole goddamn profession is based. Oh, Jesus, I don't want to go over all this again."

"May I remind you that we are talking about murder? More. That special kind of murder that is political assassination. Is that trivial? Is that trivial, damn it?!"

"No, it isn't. Why in hell do you think I came to you? It's a one-in-a-thousand chance, and I still came to you because I sure as hell do not take it lightly. I did not then expect you to treat me like a fucking foreign agent and risk the reputations, and damn it, the lives—and I mean the lives—of twenty innocent other patients on a goddamn iffy, outside chance."

Both men were tired. The words were no different; they had lost even the energy to rephrase the arguments. It was Baker who brought it to a resolution.

"Look, I'm beat, I've got to get back to Washington. If I leave now I can just catch the eleven o'clock shuttle. What can we do?"

"You must promise me that you'll take the bugs, the tapes and everything out. Otherwise I'll simply close my office and find some excuse for taking time off. Even if you do, I'll not be able to trust you completely, and I've already made arrangements to have a weekly electronic survey of my office."

"If I do what you ask, what will I get in return?"

"What do you want?"

"If there is any more talk, particularly if there is any specific plan, I want the name of the person, the date and your full co-operation in the prevention of the crime. Do I have your word?"

"You have my word."

"Then it's a deal."

The time was short and neither man was emotionally prepared for socializing. After a minimum of small talk, Baker left the office. Peter Moss sat at his desk for a few minutes and noticed that his hands were sweating profusely. He wondered if Skip had perceived it, and then he realized that he could not even remember whether they had shaken hands on parting. He was astounded at himself. He had lied with a kind of sincerity and conviction that he would have thought possible only of a psychopathic liar. Goddamn it, he thought, I won't tell that bastard a thing! Not now I won't! Would I have without this? he wondered. I don't know. My God, I'll never know, he thought.

Baker walked to the corner of Fifth Avenue, entered the cab sitting in front of the side entrance to the Guggenheim Museum with its off duty lights on. He got in, said to the driver, "We'll have to cut the electronic surveillance. He was tipped, and he's going to check."

"It's going to be very tough," said the driver.

"They did it in the old days. We'll have to do it the hard way. We'll simply have to increase the manpower. We'll check everyone going in and out of the office. Get someone on the floor. We may even have to paint the goddamn building. It's the only cover I can think of right now. Fortunately, psychoanalysts don't have many patients. We ought to be able to pick up by direct surveillance the names and addresses of most of his patients."

"I don't think that will be too hard, but once we have them, what do we know? Which ones? With the thin evidence we have to go on, does it warrant the expense of tracking all of them?"

"I don't know," said Baker. "It probably doesn't. But I think we better do it."

"Do you think if it is a real threat there is any chance he'll tell you?"

"I don't know," said Baker. "He is now convinced that he will *never* tell me; but if and when it is a real threat, I suspect he will come around. Of course, we will not depend on it."

Chapter XIX

March—four months before the convention

McAllister was furious.

"Jesus, Kate. How could you have done it? What the hell is the matter with you? You know damn well that you are seen as my absolute surrogate. If you were caught running nude through Central Park, it might just as well be me. People know our relationship. They know that you speak for me; that you have authority to represent me, and when you do something it's as though I had done it. How could you? How could you do this without first consulting me?"

Lincoln McAllister had just read in the morning paper that Kate Parr had visited Elizabeth Hilton in the hospital. The columns were filled with the speculation that this represented a rapprochement between McAllister and Hilton. It had been done without his knowledge, and had been done on the recommendation—no, that was too strong a word—on the subtle suggestion of Hugh Baker that "it might be a kindness to visit poor Elizabeth in what are obviously the terminal stages of her illness."

She knew exactly how it would be interpreted by the press, but after a month of waiting for Link to make his promised "gesture," she decided that she would make it for him. He would have been even more furious if he had known that an old-fashioned bouquet of spring flowers was sitting in a place of honor on Elizabeth Hilton's bedstand with a note prominently displaying his forged signature attached to it. She deemed it wise not to mention it at this time.

"Link, she's a dying woman. She's not responsible for her husband's deeds. I felt sorry for her. Was it so terrible to indulge in a small act of decency and generosity to the one who is probably Roger Hilton's chief victim."

"I'm touched. I'm truly touched," Link responded with rare sarcasm. "Who the hell do you think you're talking to? What are you giving me this lady's tea bullshit for? Who are you—a member of her garden club; a former classmate at Foxcroft perhaps? Goddamn it, Kate, you are me! It was Lincoln McAllister visiting that woman! It was Lincoln McAllister embracing Roger Hilton through the body of his dying wife."

"Yes, it was," she said finally, exasperated. "So what?"

He was stunned. Her last remarks were a direct confrontation. She had never spoken in those terms to him and, for that matter, neither had he to her. It was as close to a direct challenge as had ever been issued between them. For a moment their relationship was at its most precarious. Fortunately, a lifetime of control restrained him from any impulsive gesture. He sat quietly for a moment.

She was also silent, shocked at the direct confrontation. She had always "handled" Link when he was at his most difficult. Ultimata were not her style with anyone, least of all with him, and she recognized that she had come dangerously close to a take-it-or-leave-it statement. She knew that she must retreat.

"Link, we have been waiting patiently. All of us. Hugh Baker, Horace Mudd, Lowell Stoneham. Even Jack Wentworth called me, saying, 'Link has got to do something.' Everyone waiting for Link to do something. Finally, I couldn't stand it any longer. Perhaps it's my fragility. I decided you had to do something and if you couldn't do it, I could do it for you. Is that so terrible? Is that so terrible, Link?"

He did not respond.

She continued, "What was the alternative? To let the nomination go down the drain. Link, I swear to you, if you had not made the gesture, they would have dumped you. With all the preparation, they would have dumped you. It would have meant that your own ego was too large to play the game. It had nothing to do with the film. I have been assured by Baker that that film will never be used. Link, Horace Mudd, himself, called you! He is not a man who does those things. He delegates authority. Horace Mudd called you because he wanted you to have the absolute assurance that whatever happened between you and Jim Doyle no longer had existence. Somehow or other—I do not know; I do not care to know—it is to be taken care of. He is a man who commands the details of life, and I trust that command. If Mudd were not sure, would he be planning to rebuild the party around you? Think about it, Link. The Doyle exposures bothered him not one whit! But your refusal to get off your sanctimonious butt offended him. You cannot afford to offend Horace Mudd! I could not afford to let you do it, so I took things into my own hands—for the first time, Link—and made the gesture for you."

"You're making me think it was a favor you did me. The next thing you'll be expecting is my gratitude."

"You're goddamn right it was a favor, and perhaps we should stop the hypocrisy. You wanted me to do it. You had too much pride to do it yourself. You wanted it done, without having to do it—and that's effectively what I did. You wanted it done, Link. And you might as well face it. I would not have moved if I didn't know for a certainty that you wanted it done."

His face flushed with anger, and he was about to say something irretrievable and final when slowly the anger abated as the recognition gradually emerged that she was right. He had wanted her to do it! He wanted to be President more than anything in the world. He wanted the opportunity to serve, but beyond that, he knew more fully now than ever, he wanted the romance, the excitement, the power, the prestige, the trappings, the vanity, the whole works that he had tried for so long to deny. Yes, he thought quietly, he *had* wanted her to do it. He had been waiting for her to do it.

Chapter XX

April—three months before the convention

ELIZABETH HILTON DEAD
(Headline, New York *Daily News*)

Sarah had left Adam in the bedroom and had gone to her desk to try to bring some structure to the shambles of their household finances. She had always hated petty bills and accounts and neglected them until the last moment. Her career was, to put it kindly, in a state of suspension, and she daily blessed the understanding of her partners. Fortunately much of her work could be done by phone, and she had installed an extra line in the apartment.

She sorted through the overdue statements, some

still unopened, as she maintained a steady and continuous prattle of small talk. She knew Adam enjoyed it, although she doubted that he listened. His perfunctory "uh-hums," "sures" and "yeses" were simply a counterpoint that gave the feeling of communication across the rooms, bridging the barrier of vision, space and even divided attentions.

Suddenly she stopped the mechanical conversation—not even herself aware of what she had been saying—interrupted by a rush of panic. What was that? she asked herself. And even as she asked, she recognized that what had intruded so dramatically and terrifyingly on the typical evening ritual was the silence in the other room. The absolute silence.

She started abruptly to get up, and thought she couldn't move. Her hands were gripped tightly into the desk, holding her down. I must get up, she said to herself. And then, as though Indian wrestling with herself, she found herself frozen in a state of isometric tension and nonmovement. He's dead, she thought. I know it, he's lying there stretched out dead while I've been prattling on. "He's dead," she said, this time softly and out loud.

The sound of her own voice brought her back to reality and she found she could control her own limbs and actually rise from the chair. She saw the nude, pale body stretched hairless and waxy, more like a mannequin than a cadaver. His body was perfused with sweat and she noticed with agony and relief the blood pulsating through the swollen left kneecap. He was half propped up on a pillow and his head had fallen to the side on his left shoulder. The blue and white Yankee baseball cap had been pushed to the side across one eye, making him look even more like a little boy.

"Adam," she called softly. He stirred briefly but reassuringly. He was in that drugged stupor that approximated sleep. She started to remove the cap and realized how seldom he took it off. Originally, he had bought the cap, out of vanity, to wear out of doors, since he was now almost totally bald from the combination of chemotherapy and radiation. But the cap had become a habit and a conceit beyond the purposes of vanity.

He hated being bald and he wore it now even in the house.

Sarah noticed that in the few months he had stopped treatment a fuzz of new hair was developing. How long would it take, she wondered, for a full, new head of hair? Too long, she thought. Too long, she knew for a certainty. She allowed herself the luxury of crying, quietly so as not to disturb him. It was now apparent that left to its own devices the disease would complete its pillage of his body within four to six months at the most. The doctors had told him as much, and for once they were right. But Adam, she knew, would not wait for the end. He had that dreadful ritual! What did it mean? Although confined to a wheelchair most of the time, he forced himself each day to walk a measured hundred feet, five times the length of their living room each night, using only his crutches. She begged him not to do it, but he persisted with pain and sweat and muffled cries. It was part of some crazy ritual of survival. She had no idea why he insisted on doing it—masochistically putting himself through this ordeal—but in her heart she suspected that the day he would not be able to carry out the macabre ritual he would kill himself.

She gently pulled the sheet over his body and considered the irony of their relationship. When they had met, he was a boy to her, only a child; and through her he had become a man and her lover; and now he was once again not just a child, but her child. And she, at thirty-three, she who had vaguely assumed that some day she would have children was forced to endure the agonies of a death of a child before experiencing the birth.

She was particularly vulnerable today, as she always was after the visit with his parents. They were good and kind people and she had long since ceased to be embarrassed by her relationship with their son. But their persistent imprecations, their pleading with her—as though she had any more control over this willful child than they had—tore her apart. In great part they were so reasonable and rational; they only wanted him back in treatment and under medical supervision.

How in hell, Sarah wondered, had they found out that he had stopped treatment? Is nothing sacred any more? What happened, she wondered, to that bullshit concept of patient-doctor confidentiality? He was an adult and deserved the dignity of an adult, which included the right of privacy. And even as she thought it she realized that she was now constantly angry with the doctors, at the same time feeling fully aware that the ostensible reasons were only rationalizations for her rage at their impotence in the face of his illness. If not now, sooner or later Adam would be reduced to a nonautonomous, undignified lump, and then his parents could come and claim, by right of kinship, possession of their still living son.

They begged her to use her influence with Adam to have him come home, not alone but with her, to ease her burden as well as his. Her influence, she thought ironically. What influence? He had the fierce stubbornness of an adolescent, intensified by his commitment to "the plan." That fucking plan, she thought. He was still convinced that somehow or other he would dignify his death by some heroic action. She had long ceased trying to talk him out of it when she became aware of the fact that he was physically incapable of carrying out any dramatic action, and when she also realized any positive calculations, any future planning, regardless of how destructive or how unrealistic, served as a pagan dying ritual. They gave meaning to his passive moments.

But then there were the times when she was afraid he *would* carry it out. He was so ingenious, so persistent. Sarah knew the job at the flower stand in Grand Central was part of "the plan." Every day, in the wheelchair, on the lower level of the concourse, from four to seven, he sold flowers at the small flower shop alongside Track 113, where the Hudson River trains departed. She never did find out how he got the job but she knew why. She didn't have to ask him. Roger Hilton commuted regularly from those trains and it was part of "the plan." He was getting paranoid about the plan.

One week ago he reported that Hilton had actually stopped and bought a carnation from him, jauntily putting it into his lapel. He reported with delight that with Hilton's usual physical ineptitude, he had managed to lose it in the brush of the crowd before he had even entered the gate.

"I could have killed him right then and there if I only had a forty-five," he had said. "But now he may never stop for another carnation. Not after the last bravura attempt ended so dismally. And then again, if I had had the forty-five, he might never have stopped the first time."

It is conceivable, she thought, he could do it. He was so imaginative and so damn stubborn. She knew he wanted to do it and there were times she was terrified that against all odds, he *would* do it.

And then again, there were times when she wanted him to!

Chapter XXI

April—same day

The plan had been to meet in town the following morning at Stephen Cross's apartment at the Ritz Towers, but at the last minute Roger Hilton had called him demanding that he come up to the country that night. Stephen Cross didn't like the tone—or its implications. Perhaps demanding was too strong, he thought, perhaps it was simply the urgency of time—less than three months before the convention—combined with the singular change that Elizabeth Hilton's death had effected on Hilton's behavior. Grief took many forms, he knew, but he had never seen this one. It was as though all the gloss had been removed from a piece of furniture:

stains, varnishes and waxes and polishes. What remained was a raw wood surface. Only here, the defects were not pretty, the graining was too wild and uncontrolled. The rough, imperfect construction too evident. The man seemed—not to have gone to pieces—but to have come together in a singularity that was almost a caricature of himself. His swings were no longer out of moodiness into good humor, but from despair into a manic aggressiveness that was somewhat frightening. For the first time, Stephen Cross began to have some doubts about Killer Whale.

He was still convinced it was absolutely essential. Whatever the man's defects, they were no different, Cross insisted, from those of other successful leaders. He was pilloried by the damn liberal, intellectual community, who would have adored, indeed did adore the same tricks when performed by FDR. Cross vas an unreconstructed Hilton booster. He offered n apologies for The Scandal and, with the cool precision that was his trademark, he would marshal his evidence and present a litany of achievements that when articulated through his brilliant, logical and eloquent legal mind could challenge the hostility of even the most rabid anti-Hiltonian.

McAllister was a fool. A victory was essential, but to "win" by capitulation to the left wing of the party, would be a Pyrrhic victory indeed. Hilton would be the instrument for recapturing the party by its legitimate heirs. Cross alone, in that small coterie that was the privy council of Red Herring, recognized the possibility for using the brilliantly conceived design as a blueprint for an entirely different construction. It was he, then, who first proposed to Jim Doyle that Red Herring be used as an authentic political move for power, rather than a mere sociological redeeming of Hilton's public image.

If Hilton were to be forced to serve McAllister, and all that he stood for, Cross would make sure that there would be a quid pro quo. McAllister would also be serving the principles of the right wing, whose instrument Hilton had been. Red Herring would become Killer Whale. Red Herring was foolproof; it had the simplicity of genius. Cross assumed, therefore, it would work independent of its intended goals.

There was, of course, the fact and presence of Horace Mudd. Mudd did not play losing hands. If Mudd were behind something, it not only could succeed, it had to succeed. He did not relish the role of Mudd as an adversary, but then Mudd would not know until it was too late. And then, of course, they would play their cards judiciously and slowly. In that way it would be fait accompli before Mudd was even aware. Once power was achieved—all the rules changed.

Besides, he thought, Mudd is an old man. How old is he? he wondered. Good God, sooner or later the man has to die. And Cross smiled to himself, realizing that he was wishing that he would die, and in that wish he exposed how frightened he still was of the Admiral. But aren't we all? he thought.

Cross had been driving up the Sawmill River Parkway in Hilton's oversized black twelve-year-old Cadillac. The car had been sent by Hilton as a gesture of conciliation and respect. Cross hardly noticed as the driver turned off the parkway and made his way through local roads. The car came suddenly to a halt, breaking the flow of Cross's thoughts. He had only been to Briarcliff once before, and then during the day. He had not then noticed the large, closed gates at the entrance to the property, nor had he been aware there was a guard at the gate. Was this new, he wondered, or simply the difference between nighttime security and daytime? The house itself was an incredibly ugly and pretentious late Victorian mansion, on an extraordinarily beautiful piece of property completely surrounded by stone walls. The thirty-four-acre estate was like one of many built along the Hudson as summer homes by Jay Gould and the like at the turn of the century to enhance their self-images as medieval barons and lords of the manor. Impossibly expensive to maintain, most of them had been abandoned or willed for tax purposes to small church colleges or local communities to serve as historic sites and museums. Hilton had invested the windfall profits from the sale of his three books of memoirs in this retreat and the property in South Carolina. The appreciation of land values had been so grotesque that even this white elephant had enhanced the ever growing estate of Roger Hilton. Stephen Cross thought how ironic that since his public disgrace and banishment from public life, every decision of Hilton's seemed to have a charmed success about it. His loss of power and respectability seemed to be accompanied by the perverse compensation of an accretion of great wealth. Now that the respectability and power would be restored, he would be a force to be reckoned with, and Stephen Cross, as his sole link with the outside networks of the right-wing establishment, would guide and control this power.

He was met at the door by Jim Doyle, who took his bag and ushered him into a little study next to the library. A small table had been set for three with a light supper. During dinner Cross laid out the current progress of Killer Whale, née Red Herring. Jim Doyle was extraordinarily quiet and withdrawn, unlike his traditional ebullience at these small occasions. Doyle had changed in the last few months. He had withdrawn into himself and the ready humor which seemed formerly in inexhaustible supply was now, while still pleasant, subdued and more likely to be tinged with irony. It must be hard on him, Cross realized. With Elizabeth Hilton's death, the two men were now almost always alone and the burden of Hilton's self-pity and anger was a heavy cross even for as devoted a man as Doyle.

The meeting had been arranged to review, for one final time, the few remaining plans until the convention, and to begin to outline general strategy for the post-election period. Cross continued explicating the agenda throughout dinner with little interruption from Hilton. By the time the brandy and cigars had been passed, he anxiously began to wonder what urgency had demanded his arrival in Briarcliff this evening. He had patiently waited for Hilton to make his move. It was Hilton's show and Cross knew better than to impose his own timetable on it.

"We really pulled it off, Steve," said Roger Hilton.

"Better than any of us had a right to anticipate, Mr.

President," responded Cross, who persisted in using this form of address that he had used in his eight years as presidential adviser.

"I'm glad you agree with me, Steve, because now I feel there is no reason to keep to the original timetable. We must move faster."

"What do you mean, Mr. President? We have from the beginning known that patience is essential. That time is on our side."

"Time is on nobody's side. Since Elizabeth's death I've realized that. I'm not going to fuck around eating all this shit for the next ten years and then drop dead before I've had my chance."

"It's not a matter of ten years."

"I don't give a shit how many years," Hilton continued, his voice rising. "I want to move faster."

His speech was slurred, as it tended to be after drinking. Cross noticed, somewhat too late, that the conversation started after a dangerous amount of wine had been consumed over dinner. He looked up briefly, trying to catch Doyle's eyes for some sign of what was coming. Doyle quickly averted his gaze. Cross was now wary. It was crucial to calm the man down.

"You may be right, Mr. President, and I do think we can adjust the entire timetable. As soon as the election is in the bag, I see no reason why we can't begin to make our moves on the administration."

"I've already begun to make my moves," Hilton said with a smirk.

"You've what?" asked Cross incredulously. It had been a firm, and he had assumed inviolate, condition of the whole Killer Whale Operation that neither Cross nor Hilton, and by implication Doyle, would make a move without prior consultation.

"Jesus, Roger," he said, slipping into the familiarity he normally did not allow. "Don't tell me you've seen McAllister."

"As good as," Hilton said enigmatically.

Cross turned with controlled rage to Doyle.

"You went to see him, despite our agreement, despite the pledge we had taken that no moves would be made without prior consultation."

Hilton recognized the anger even under the self-control, and the show of anger ignited his own.

"Who the fuck do you think you're talking to? When you're talking to Jim Doyle you're talking to me. Do you understand that? Who the hell are you to lecture me? And since when does the President of the United States have to raise his hand to any man to ask permission to take a piss? Fuck you and your consultation bullshit. When the going was rough I made the decisions. Me, alone. And when they were good, I exulted in that, knowing it was I who had the balls and was ready to put them on the line. And when the going got rough it was my balls that were chopped off, not yours. You sat in your fat, fucking office in Wall Street continuing to pull in the money, continuing to be the respectable Stephen Cross, while I was being shit on by every pimp and power merchant who used to wait in line to kiss my ass before. Don't you lecture me!"

Cross realized that he had to stall for time, to allow Hilton to calm down. He knew Hilton's moods and he also knew Doyle had means of ameliorating them. He endured the tirade even when it became personally humiliating. He had endured them many times before when Hilton was President and things had begun to go wrong. He was a trained conciliator, and as he moved to regain control over himself he regained control over the situation. In time Hilton calmed down.

"Perhaps we ought to get explicit. Could you give me some idea of what changes in the timetable you had in mind, Mr. President?"

"Give it to him, Jim," Hilton said to Doyle.

Doyle produced a small binder with two typewritten pages which Stephen Cross proceeded to read carefully and slowly. He compared the agenda against the originally agreed upon timetable. The modifications essentially accelerated Hilton's political revival. The original plan had simply been to go along with Red Herring in every detail up until the election, thereby moving Hilton into a position of social respectability. He would assume the role of elder statesman, but distinctly a retired elder statesman. The increased respectability would allow for his gradual utilization in ceremonial positions within the party, and administrative positions in philanthropic and neutral roles. The closest to any position of political importance that was planned was his ultimate assignment to a major role with the UN.

Hilton persisted in being a hero in the Third World and among the Communist powers. Consistent with its tradition, it was assumed that the UN would be more than happy to trade principles for power. Once Hilton was no longer a danger to the UN, they would appraise him as a man whose eminent corruptibility made him a worthy member of their club.

The key difference in the current agenda was that the political moves would now parallel the social ones. Cross was relieved to notice what he assumed was the modifying influence of Jim Doyle. The tempo was still, thank God, slow. The post-election part, Cross could still live with, although he began to realize that he himself had no time to lose in beginning putting his clamp on Hilton. He must not let this genie completely out of the bottle. He knew that now, and internally berated himself for having forgotten it even for a moment. The one sticking point was the flagrant public move prior to the election. Fortunately, there was only one such prominent step and that was that Hilton was now demanding for himself a role in the nominating convention. It would, of course, immediately alert Mudd. Baker, then, would start the machinery in operation, and Cross was wise enough to be frightened that this time he, too, might be ground in the gears of that powerful engine. He never underestimated Baker.

On the other hand, the whole thing was impossible. McAllister would never allow it. He gingerly started the discussion by cleverly conceding the rightness of moving into the political sphere immediately after the election and agreeing with 90 per cent of the revisions.

"The only real reservation that I have, Mr. President, is on the role in the convention. I'm not saying we could not manage it, but it would have to be cleared with McAllister and I don't think that would wash."

"So you think it would have to be cleared with McAllister; and you don't think it would wash," said

Hilton, the humiliating repetition of words suggesting his contempt.

"But you know McAllister." Cross continued, confused by the open contempt, which signaled a serious change in the relationship between Hilton and himself. "McAllister is cautious. He lacks the courage for such a move. I don't think you will be able to talk him into it."

"I don't have to talk that tightass fag into anything," said Hilton. He was smiling now, not angry. "From now on I have stopped asking. I'm telling, again. And I'm telling you now—that pretty boy is going to put his cock *wherever* I tell him to, *whenever* I tell him to."

The assurance, the absolute authority with which this was said stunned Cross. He was suddenly aware that a whole game had been played out without his being a participant. He turned quizzically to Doyle and for the first time Doyle looked at him directly.

"McAllister will go along, Steve," Doyle said quietly.

"He's agreed already," Cross continued. It was an acknowledgment now, no more a question, and with the slight affirmative nod from Jim Doyle, Stephen Cross realized for the first time that he'd "been moved out of the board room." From now on he would be given administrative assignments and messenger boy service. But when Hilton made his major moves Cross would not be directing them. He'd lost the game.

Where had he miscalculated? He prided himself on his capacity to analyze data. It was McAllister's resistance to Hilton that had placed Cross so confidently in the key position. The one thing he had counted on was McAllister's hatred and contempt for Hilton. This was the pivotal ingredient that made Cross a necessary broker between these two contending forces. And now an accommodation between the two of them had been reached. Some unpredictable quirk, some unanalyzable piece of data had made him dispensable. He realized now that he was on the way out of the game. An uncontrolled Hilton could be truly dangerous, and he was surprised to find that he was almost relieved to be moving to the sidelines. Whatever Hilton's moves, Cross would no longer be responsible. Perhaps it was better that way. But he had his work cut out for him. He would have to carry out Hilton's plans scrupulously, while easing himself out of the picture. He dare not antagonize him. Not now, when he, himself, had been responsible for preparing once again Hilton's access to the summit of power. With a runaway train there must inevitably be suffering, injury and damage. Just as well not to be driving the locomotive. It was a good time, he thought wearily, to retire from politics.

Chapter XXII

May—two months before the convention

> Roger Hilton attended the graduation exercises at New York Theological Seminary, where his son was ordained an Episcopal minister. On entering the auditorium, the ex-President was given a standing ovation. (New York *Times*)

Adam was sitting in a wheelchair facing Peter Moss. It had been a few weeks since he had stopped trying to move from the wheelchair to the armchair, recognizing the futility of a move that only served appearances.

"After all, Doctor," he had said, "there ought to be no 'appearances' in a psychoanalytic office. Unless," he said whimsically, "there is nothing but appearances. Besides, I must conserve my energy for more important things."

Something was different. Moss was aware of it from the minute he saw Adam come in from the waiting room. The blue baseball cap looked even looser and more ludicrous on his head. His face was progressively beginning to look like the porcelain face of a Victorian doll that could have been a girl or a boy; either or neither; a neutral look. Yet superimposed on the clear childish image was something else, something complex and frightening. Too much morphine? A sudden turn for the worse in the illness? Moss didn't know, but he was aware of a transition, and at this stage of Adam's illness, any change was not for the good. The boy looked different and even though he didn't know how, he didn't like it and he was scared. His fears were given solid grounding when Adam started by saying, "I had thought of trying the couch today."

It had been months since he had been able to maneuver the couch, or, indeed, since there had been any purpose to it.

"Why do you say that?" Moss asked.

Adam ignored his question and said, "I think what I will do is simply turn my chair around so that we are not facing each other. It will be like the old days. I want that today."

Then he continued as though it were a typical Monday session. His usual preoccupations with pain, death and the awareness of the limits of time left to him followed, and, as always, were generously sprinkled with his uniquely dry form of gallows humor. Typically, too, there was the gentle baiting and teasing of Moss which served as Adam's reserved equivalent of expressions of affection. The only noticeable difference between this Monday and the many that immediately preceded it was the information that Adam had spent the entire weekend in Brewster with his family. Moss's curiosity was piqued. During these final months of his life Adam had cherished his time with Sarah—selfishly closing out even those others who loved him. His family reluctantly respected this decision, and put no pressure on him.

Moss wondered why this weekend was different. Was there an event, a birthday, an anniversary he had forgotten? He thought not. There was the vague sense of something new, something out of order, which erupted brutally as Adam said, "I think this had best be our last meeting."

Moss tensed in his fear. There was a short pause and he said, "Are things ... very, very bad, Adam?"

"Things have been very 'bad' for such a long time, Doctor, but they will now be brought to an end."

Moss had assumed that the boy would not last through the summer and thought he was prepared for his suicide. He knew that over the last year he had supplied him with enough drugs, that by culling from daily usage, Adam could have saved more than enough to kill himself ten times over, and yet, now that the inevitable seemed at hand, Moss was unprepared.

Needing to say something and not knowing what to say or what could be said, and recognizing that even something foolish was better than nothing, he asked: "You don't think we should just finish out the week?"

"I think I *will* finish out the week, but without you, if you don't mind. Not that I'm not grateful. I did want to say that. My God, I guess my therapy has been successful. I'm able to pay a compliment without adding an ironic note or even a touch of sarcasm. I am grateful, Doctor, I am truly grateful. Be comforted—I would like to continue to the very end. I would like to feel this process and your presence were somehow with me at the end. And I do like being with you, but while your 'woods are lovely, dark and deep,' I do have 'promises to keep, and miles to go before I sleep.'"

"Adam, what are you trying to say to me?"

Adam had not talked about either the assassination or Roger Hilton, for that matter, for the past five to six weeks, and Peter Moss had simply assumed that fatigue, pain and the burdens of time had made the fantasy too remote—or if not too distant—simply uninteresting. But now he realized something quite different. The failure to discuss the fantasies did not mean the abandonment of them but rather that they had reached a termination point, that the fantasies, at least to Adam's exhausted and drugged mind, were no longer necessary, because they had assumed a delusional reality of their own. With a jolt, Moss realized the boy had prepared some pathetic Götterdämmerung.

"My God, Adam, not that crazy assassination business. Not Roger Hilton again. There's no way you could do it. And I don't mean just psychologically, although I think I know you well enough to know that you could not carry it through in cold blood. But, Adam, look at yourself. There is no way you could do it physically."

"Doctor, you are *so* wrong. There are many ways that I could do it. Let me suggest just one. The first thing that is important in an assassination is to know one's victim. I know Roger Hilton very well. I have already established the first essential ingredient of any assassination—a predictable place for the event to occur. Hilton is an obsessive, a ritualistic man, almost a mechanical man, and despite himself, he is bound to a schedule. It must have made it very hard for the Secret Service to guard him when he was President. I know how they like alternate routes and such. At any rate, he isn't President and there is no more Secret Service. Or is there? I hadn't thought of that. But never mind. It's unimportant. The first thing, as I said, is location. There are at least three that are feasible. He has taken to appearing in public, you know, with a great show. It goes along with the media hype. I can't believe that even you aren't now aware that there is a conspiracy to re-establish this man's bona fides in the public mind, if not in their hearts.

"Well, the papers are filled with the son of a bitch, and each time he appears in print a little more of the shit is washed away. And now, all of a sudden, we are exposed to the 'man of the people.' Not just formal and occasional public appearances. Now, he's a regular diner at Twenty-one! The table right at the head of the stairs. The whores who run that joint are ready to have him right back. Did you know that he eats there regularly? Wednesday lunches. That's one place. But, of course, although Roger Hilton has no difficulty getting into Twenty-one, I would. They wouldn't want a freaky cripple disturbing their clientele.

"Then, of course, there's Tuesday night at the opera. He really is not a great opera fan. He goes, like most of that Tuesday night crowd, because he enjoys being *thought of* as an opera lover. I find he dislikes Mozart and Wagner and is inclined to either skip these performances or leave early. I can forgive him the Wagner, but can you imagine attending the opera and skipping out on Mozart? I see him there quite regularly. He tries not to see me. He averts his glance when I come into sight. He doesn't like cripples. I think that because of my wheelchair he assumes I have some horrible deformity. He doesn't know that all that's wrong with me is that like everyone else in this world I am part of the process of dying.

"So you see, Doctor, there is a second locus; but the crowds, the unpredictability of intermissions and attendance make it too chancy. I suppose a cleverer person—or a healthier person—could have managed it there. There is a kind of romance about death in the opera! Hitchcock certainly enjoyed the idea. But, then, for a routine man like Hilton—and myself, for that matter—the best plan should involve routine.

"He commutes. And there, with the exception of when he is collecting another one of his fucking honors, he's regular. Oh, is he a regular commuter! If only the New York Central could live up to that man's punctuality. Occasionally on Monday, Tuesday and Wednesday, but *every* Thursday and Friday that man catches the Hudson River train out of Manhattan at six-oh-seven. And every Thursday and Friday I sit there and watch him. I did tell you, didn't I, Doctor, that I had taken this job at the flower stand in Grand Central Station? Did you know, Doctor, that it's right outside of Track One-thirteen? Right there where the large lower level station tunnels down into the two or three end tracks that service the Hudson River Division."

The job, that idiotic job, thought Moss with alarm. The one piece of inexplicable behavior, in a man like Adam, who never did anything without reasons. Moss had speculated over that job for weeks, knowing that it had some purpose, some meaning beyond the vague explications offered by Adam, until finally out of sheer frustration and exhaustion he had ceased trying to find out. And then, he had simply forgotten it.

Moss was shaken and upset. He did not usually forget details. Not forgotten—repressed? He did not want to remember it. He did not want to know. Why? Was this a defense against complicity in something? Did his unconscious know?

"You remember that dream, Doctor," Adam continued. "You know the dream I mean—the one in the railroad station. The nightmare of impotence and agony. My old familiar dream which always repeats with only the locale changed. The last time I had that dream it was in a railroad station. I thought it was Grand Central. You do remember that, Doctor?

"I now understand prophetic dreams. Dreams never predict the future, they only direct it. We know what we want to do, and we don't know that we know, and our dreams direct our behavior. Dreams don't reflect life, it is life that reflects the dream.

"I remember that dream," Adam continued, "and all of your comments. The stupid business of the hand grenade, and your pointing out how diffuse a weapon it was. Still, I knew that there must be a way. There had to be a way to snuff out Roger Hilton like a cockroach. The world needs Hilton out of the way. And even if it doesn't, if I have only deluded myself, I need to eliminate him.

"But I could not take an innocent life. An efficient mode was needed, and what is more precise than the proficient sniper. A rifle, such a nice, exact instrument, particularly at close range. At fifty feet even an amateur becomes an expert, and I'm no amateur. No more. No more indeed. No, a rifle is much better than the automatics. The Uzi is for movies, and movie heroes—strong, brawny men with heavy biceps and limber limbs.

"The rifle is admittedly awkward in a crowd. You can, however, shorten the barrel on a rifle without too much difficulty, and without too much loss of accuracy at short ranges. Did you know that, Doctor? It becomes, I suppose, like a long pistol. And then if you can add an expensive gunsight, your precision is greatly enhanced. There are still some advantages to being a crippled boy; there's a look of innocence about the weak and dying."

Moss listened, incredulous, as Adam described his visiting a gunsmith in Yonkers. Adam had developed a simple, yet credible story of being a hunting and shooting fan since childhood—but now, his strength gone, he was denied the pleasures of a lifetime in the last few years left to him. Of course, the gunsmith helped him. Who could resist the appeal of this tragic young man?

"He helped me with the basic design. Between the two of us we designed the weapon. It looks funny, but it's light enough in weight so even a cripple can raise it to his shoulder. I feel sorry about the gunsmith. I wouldn't want him to get into trouble. I want you to know just what he did and why. Out of kindness and ignorance he was helping an invalid continue squirrel hunting as he had ever since he was a boy. My God, I never hunted anything in my life!"

"But what good is a rifle, even an accurate, deadly rifle, in a place like Grand Central?" Moss interrupted. "Even a foreshortened one would be detected. And surely you know you can't trust the steadiness of your hands. Adam, it's bad enough killing someone you think deserves it—but would you risk the innocent?"

"If you're ever in Grand Central, Doctor, take a look at the flower stall. I added a few things, a couple of old Victorian plant stands. I think they were intended for ferns. Now they're covered with trailing plants for sale. Firm, steady things, those stands are like tripods. You could mount that gun I just described to you (prepared for 'squirrel' hunting) in the center of this tripod. It would be such an easy job. Of course, one would need an adjustable mount, something easily and quickly maneuvered. I have an old telescope—ideal for the purposes. Did you ever own a telescope, Doctor? They're fine, rotating, pivotal, well-calibrated instruments, really if anything too elegant and precise for these purposes; you would never even have to use the fine tuning. With just a touch of the fingertips you could rotate that gun around and point it at any target. When not in use you could keep the gun mounted vertically, and it would be hidden by the trailing plants.

"Would you believe that I've had one there for three weeks and no one ever noticed? The stand itself is so ornate. But what is even more remarkable is that I've actually pointed that gun at my target. I've had him in my sights five times already. I could have killed him at any time but *I* wasn't ready to die yet. I thought I was, but I always wanted one more day. Up until now I always prepared to endure the pain for one more day. Now there are no more days.

"You'll be pleased, Doctor, that I've not been reckless. An elephant gun would be surer, perhaps, but then, so would a grenade, and you pointed out the dangers in that to the innocent."

It was the second time, Moss noticed, that Adam had mentioned his complicity by warning him against the grenade. Was Adam taunting him? Moss was unnerved. In a horrible sense everything—every damn logical thing he had told Adam to convince him of the impossibility of an assassination, had simply been used by him to make a plan that was more feasible. In a perverse way Adam had converted him into a coauthor of the scenario.

"I remember from court hearings," Adam continued, "that a bullet can go through one body and enter another. It terrified me for a time. How can one protect against that? I know that I can get him in my line of sight without anyone in front of him, but what about *behind* him? Could I be that sure? Am I that aware of trajectory? The twenty-two is a more conservative, a more socially responsible weapon. I feel relieved with it. Are you aware of the twenty-two caliber murders that have been going on? The Cosa Nostra seems to prefer them nowadays. Perhaps it's an economy drive. Close up they seem to be as effective as the big boys. I do run a risk; he may not die. But I would plan on hitting him right between the eyes. With the rifle's velocity and as close a range as I'm sure I could get, I think my chances would be good.

"So you see, Doctor, there is at least one way that I could do it. That is, of course," he continued with a smile, "*if* I were so inclined."

"Adam," Moss interrupted, "why are you doing this? Why are you playing games with me? What is the purpose of all this? Will it please you if I admit I am thoroughly confused, and, beyond that, more than a little frightened. All right then—I am. But what are you trying to do?"

"I don't want to discuss it any more. I'm going to be walking out of this office in twenty minutes and I don't expect ever to see you again. I don't know how I want to end our relationship, but I know it's not this way. If I continue discussing this, I know what your response would be, and I'm not interested in hearing what you would have to say. I don't want tendentiousness now. Not at the end."

And with that, he abruptly changed subjects.

"I wish I'd had the right dream for you today. I wanted to end with a special dream. I willed the dream with all my power—but it wouldn't come. It would have added a particular element, an aesthetic completion. I wanted to dream that I was St. George and that I had finally lifted my lance to slay the dragon, and in this dream, I raised it easily, with a sense of confidence, of freedom, of power. With arms, freed from pain, I would have guided my lance like the sword of a graceful torero—true and deep into the beast.

"I willed that dream. But life is not all aesthetics. Obsessives can never completely have their way. I did have the next best thing; I finally had a dreamless sleep."

By this time Moss could feel sweat forming on his neck. He did not know what to say to his patient. He knew Adam's obstinacy, and knew he would not discuss his "plan." He was not even thinking clearly of the assassination attempt, or if it were such a thing. He would have to sort that out later. But this he did know. He *would not* see Adam again. And this was their goodby. He wanted to offer something, but he did not know what. He wished to say something wise and comforting, but there were no such words. He realized this termination was like every termination of every patient. The same incompleteness and silence and sense of loss. The same self-consciousness. Only this time the patient was not moving out of treatment into life, but into death.

"I think dreamless sleeps are the best," Moss responded. And the two of them drifted into the small talk and intellectual discussion that often marks the true conversation of dramatic times and important moments. As Adam was about to leave, he turned in his wheelchair, looked Peter Moss in the eye and said, "I've trusted you with my life, Doctor, and you have never betrayed that trust. I am now trusting you with my death."

Chapter XXIII

June 15

Friday, June 15, was raw and unseasonably ugly. It was the one fact that almost everyone would ultimately agree upon in attempting to reconstruct the events of that momentous day. It had rained from dawn to dusk and the temperature incredibly had dropped into the low fifties. For Sarah Pedersen, at least, the weather was a relief. A beautiful day would have been unbearable. She had found herself unable to control her crying—and despite Adam's injunction that he needed her alert—she had taken two Valiums. Now she had a sense of deadness that seemed consistent with the mood of the day.

She could not bear the imminence of Adam's death. She tried to comfort herself by the knowledge that, unlike others, she had been granted time to prepare for her loss. The doctors had been amazingly accurate in predicting Adam's life expectancy. She had been proud of how she had come to accept, with at least a reasonable degree of equanimity, the end of his life. She was bitter now in the awareness of her self-delusion. One can always accept tomorrow's agony because tomorrow never comes. She had known he would die "soon," which after all is not terribly different from "sometime." But now there was this inescapable exactness of his final hours, which were upon them. This was his last day. She was sure of that. And the pain was almost unbearable. Thank God it is a day for death rather than a day for life. She could not have endured clear skies and bright sunshine. There was already too much contrast and contradiction; her pain and grief demanded consonance.

Adam was also relieved by the rain. Raincoats and slouched hats would aid in securing the necessary anonymity. Everyone would look alike in the urban sea of beige poplin. He was confident and clear in his intent. His plan would work. The extraordinary cold, however, had bothered him. He wanted nothing out of the ordinary on this day. He was a man who believed in probabilities and the statistics were on his side. Only the improbable, the unlikely and the unpredictable could destroy his purpose. Because he had kept his plan simple, outrageously so, the variables were few. The statistics were on his side, with one glaring exception; there would be no second runs. This was his final hour, and it had to be now. But then, with a certain degree of comfort, he realized that in this one sense, at least, he was no different from any other assassin. His inexperience, his weakness, his immobility, all of these may have differentiated him from the ideal assassin; but they were joined in the tension of a one-time opportunity. One roll of the dice ...

It was 3:30 P.M. In silence he and Sarah made their preparations for leaving their apartment. He noticed with delight his calm clarity of mind and serenity of purpose. That was more than he had hoped for. In contrast, however, the physical pain, which often seemed to disappear in moments of high excitement—which he had prayed would happen this day—seemed more intense than ever. He did not want Sarah to notice, but in attempting to put on the raincoat without assistance, he involuntarily cried out. His one regret was that he had to bring her into this. There was no way he could handle it by himself. He needed her co-operation, and he felt reassured that the preparatory steps he had taken would protect her. He had laid the groundwork to prepare a strong defense for her against any possible charges of complicity. He did not want to hurt anyone, most of all her, and could not bear the thought that his triumph could be marred by bringing pain to her. Adam Haas never for a moment doubted that his mission would be successful.

What in God's name am I doing here? wondered Peter Moss. A rational, ordinary, conventional human being trapped in the middle of an opera. Or worse, he thought, a soap opera. The decision had been a horrible one for him. To the last moment he could not believe he would "betray" Adam; and yet he had. But to call it betrayal was to deny the complexity of his motives. If it were his son, he would have behaved the same. He could not condone a murder—and yet, and yet to the last moment he was determined not to interfere. But then that last session with Adam! What was he doing? He was making it impossible for me not to act. He was baiting me! Perhaps he really wanted to be stopped. Oh shit, Moss thought—what a sniveling psychoanalytic cop-out. He did it—not for Adam—but because he, Peter Moss, had to. And when he finally made the call, he had the sense that Skip had been prepared and waiting. Peter had demanded, as a condition of his co-operation, that he be allowed to be present. Skip had been adamant at first, but finally consented. Skip had sworn to him that the boy would not be hurt. And what could a punitive society do to him that a merciful God had not already done? Adam would never go to trial. But why am I assuming he will make the attempt? The probabilities are still against it, he thought.

He was beginning to feel hot, huddled in his raincoat, with his rain hat kept staunchly on, and those ridiculous sunglasses which he had been assured made him less recognizable, but which simply made him feel conspicuous and silly. He was standing in the dark, at the head of the steps just inside Track 113. This afforded him a clear view of the flower stand and a decent percentage of the lower concourse covering most of the entrances to the Hudson River trains. He had spent the previous evening from four to seven at precisely the same place and had slipped away, feeling like an idiot, yet incredibly relieved. He began to feel, at first hopefully, and now almost confidently, that he had behaved for once in his life by overreacting rather than denying. His incurable optimism had often led him to err in the direction of assuming that which he did not want to happen would not, and he began to slip back into the comfort of traditional and familiar mechanisms. No, nothing would happen. Now he was sure of that, and if he felt the fool, it was the most enjoyable feeling in the world. He had a sudden recognition that all would be well and a wave of ebullience rushed into consciousness, easing his anxiety, his despair—and his guilt.

Almost at that moment he spotted the figure of Roger Hilton cutting diagonally across the concourse, passing now before the Fanny Farmer candy shop, making his turn toward Track 113, with only the flower shop directly in front of him. Moss's heart began to pound. He noticed for the first time how empty the concourse seemed for a rush hour, and how self-consciously all of the people, the vendors, the commuters, seemed to be moving in an artifice of appointed rounds. It was the last clear impression he was to have of the events of that evening. First, he noticed a quick movement at the flower stand. What it was he could not tell, seeing only Adam's back with that silly baseball cap. Then a sudden, urgent moving forward and rearrangement of the flowers. The first sound he was to hear— he was sure that it was, he was to testify to that later— was the thundering crash of the vase of flowers. Tea roses, they were, he had noticed, those cheap bunches of pink, red, coral and yellow tea roses splashed against the marble floor of the station. And then, almost as if on cue, the entire station was converted to a whir of organized action with everyone converging on the flower stand, like iron filings attracted to a magnet. The seeming chaos of the crowd mobilized into a moving design with the flower stand at its center. Roger Hilton was forgotten in the rush and confusion as a man from the newsstand leaped over, almost making a flying tackle, into the flower stand, further spewing the flowers in all directions and knocking down the large display and pushing, driving the limp young flower vendor into the ground, pushing and wrestling him like a professional football team in an after-the-fact effort to crush the ball carrier into submission.

My God, they're going to kill him, thought Moss. He heard himself screaming, "Don't hurt him! Don't hurt him! Don't hurt him!"

He started running towards the stand himself and was immediately seized by two workmen who had been repairing the railing leading down to the tracks. He knew instantly that they were agents—that there had been agents planted all over.

"Let me go!" he shouted, struggling. "They promised me he wouldn't be hurt. He's a sick, fragile boy. I don't want him hurt. They promised me."

But the two stoic figures simply pinned him against the banister and wouldn't allow him to move. Tears of frustration and pain and guilt flooded into Moss's eyes as he implored the men to let him go to the fallen figure. He no longer could see what was going on in the room and all he could hear was himself screaming at the top of his lungs, "Don't hurt him. Don't hurt him, don't hurt him."

Roger Hilton had been trembling when he walked down the stairs at the eastern side of the terminal onto the lower concourse. He was not sure whether it was simply fear, or if there wasn't a measure of excitement. He was the central figure once again. The President. The entire situation was in hand. The crowd was controlled, serving *him* as it had in the past, and as it would again in the future. They had warned him that it all might be a false alarm and he had hoped, yes, he had prayed, that it would not be. It was just what he needed. It was the excitement. The front page. The heroic salvation that would wipe out the ugly stain that had smeared his life and that would not be washed away.

They had not told him how they knew, or what they knew, except that there was a reasonable anticipation of an assassination plot; that it was by an amateur, not an organized group; that there was relatively little danger to him; and that it could be handled either by arresting the potential assassin before the fact, which might indeed be difficult, or by catching him redhanded. The latter, of course, included a certain amount of risk to Roger Hilton, but would eliminate any doubts about the intention and identity of the assassin. Hilton agreed with alacrity to the latter plan, indeed, insisting upon it. The decision, they said, was his, although there seemed an almost too ready assumption that he would be co-operative.

Of all the cockeyed schemes that he and Cross had considered, and then eliminated, never once had they imagined that sheer luck would supply them with the most dramatic tool for his political resurrection: Roger Hilton, as elder statesman, heroically putting his life in danger to co-operate in the apprehension of an assassin. He would, of course (he smiled as he thought of this), plead for the life of the assassin. He enjoyed thinking of himself reading a magnanimous and compassionate letter to spare the son of a bitch's life. He was going to enjoy this. He knew it now. He walked across the concourse in a straight line to the candy shop as he had been directed. He paused to count five as he looked in the window of the shop, pivoted, and walked directly towards Track 113. He noticed the two men starting to converge towards him from different directions in the five seconds he had been staring in the shop window, thinking he recognized one as a Secret Service man who had been assigned to special duty when he was in the White House. He walked casually, the two men a few paces behind him, and then for the first time he focused on the slight, childish-looking figure in the Yankee baseball cap behind the flower stand.

They could have been no more than fifty feet from the stand when the explosive noise of the shattering vase seemed to mobilize the entire populace of the station. He saw with glee that the flower vendor had been knocked to the floor. A massive pile-up of people converged upon the fallen body. His own two bodyguards rushed forward and he was annoyed by the fact that the crowd, intervening between him and the flower stand, obstructed his view. He wanted them to kill the bastard, and he wanted to see him killed. It had worked just as Baker had assured him it would, and he sensed the victory that would go beyond anything Baker or that bastard Mudd could have anticipated. A sense of joy and power surged within him, limited only by the annoyance of not being able to see, to witness the actual subjugation of his would-be assassin. It was a small price to pay and Roger Hilton was feeling exultant, when once again his pleasure was marred by one of those small annoyances of everyday life. Someone in the crowd had been jostled, evidently losing his footing, and had fallen forward, clutching Roger Hilton for support. Hilton loathed physical contact with strangers and he turned to look with contempt at the person who, in his clumsiness, was intruding on his triumphant moment.

Chapter XXIV

June 15 (Reprise)

It was 3:30 P.M. and it was time to leave. Adam was confident and only hoped that his moment of triumph would not be marred by bringing pain to the person he loved the most. He had hoped to carry it off alone but almost from the beginning he had realized it would not be possible. He had simply not wanted to think that he might have to compromise Sarah. It was to be his triumph. It was to be good over evil, and no innocent should suffer. For, after all, he had decided it *was* a morality play and he would so construct it. He needed an accomplice. Actually two, he realized. Peter Moss was his second.

He felt bad for having deceived Moss. He wrote

him an extended note of apology. He had not sent it, of course. He had entrusted it to Sarah. She would meet with him after the excitement died down and present him with the written apology. He was terribly appreciative of Moss and wondered whether he "loved" him. Whenever he thought of love it was always in terms of the total romantic feelings he felt towards Sarah. He of course loved his parents and his sisters, but in such a way that one neither used the word nor was forced to think about it. With Moss there had been this deep, intense attachment of gratitude and affection that he now began to realize was just another form of love. Funny that he should be thinking of Moss now. Perhaps because there were all these unsaid things between them.

He had come to know Moss—really to know him—and he hated using that knowledge for duplicitous purposes. A psychoanalyst was in a difficult position. What were his responsibilities to his patient and to society? From his own standpoint, were he a psychiatrist faced with a patient about to commit a capital crime, there would be no question that he would have a personal responsibility to prevent the crime, either by convincing the patient that he must not do it or by reporting the patient to the authorities. Even if it could be rationalized as saving the patient, Adam thought.

If only he had been more careful. There had been absolutely no reason for Moss even to know about the plan. He could have been left out of it completely. Had Adam really thought that his fantasies might become reality, he would never have talked about them with such detail. There was plenty to fill those hours anyway, and while avoidance was a form of deceit, it was not of the manipulative caliber of what had later transpired. But he himself had not known when fantasy had become transformed into actuality. It was all so subtle and all so gradual. There were, first, the dreams, then the daytime preoccupation with the dreams, and then the examining of the possibilities of the dreams, and then before he knew it, they were no longer dreams. But he had talked too much and too long and the pivotal question was whether Moss had taken him seriously. Quickly, he realized that the issue went beyond that. The real question was only *when* had Moss begun to take him seriously. When Adam made his final plans for the execution; when he realized how simple it could be; and when he had allayed his internal moral compunctions, he had stopped talking to Moss about the assassination. It was then that he realized Moss was his one serious stumbling block.

At this stage of his disease, with his constant pain and his preoccupation with death, he no longer trusted his own objectivity. He began to suspect that Moss had taken him seriously before he himself was serious, and may even have reported him. He began to have the feeling of being observed. Perhaps it was projection or paranoia. At any rate, he could not take the chance. If Moss had said something, even if only casually, to the authorities, and if he were being watched, even if only as one of many suspects, he had to devise a plan which compensated for that possibility. It was too late to stop telling Moss anything related to the plan. If Moss had suspected in the beginning, and had *not* reported it then, he would know for sure when he was told that Adam was not going to see him any more. Moss would recognize the announcement of termination of treatment as an announcement of his death, and that keen analytic mind of his would begin to speculate as to whether it was to be a death by suicide or homicide, and he would behave "responsibly."

Moss knew Adam, but Adam also knew Moss. Moss would behave responsibly. He would not risk an innocent life, even if that life were by other standards not innocent. Even if it was Roger Hilton.

So to leave Moss out was impossible. Their lives were too inextricably bound with understandings and empathies, too close. He could not be excluded. A plan was needed, convincing enough for Moss to accept, yet ambiguous enough for him to have doubts as to whether it were an actual confession or simply another fantasy. Too open and honest a statement of intention might have created too great a burden for Moss to betray. Adam realized he'd have to set his trap carefully, suggesting a plot which would be effective, and yet not directly indicating his absolute intentions.

It was then he realized that Sarah would have to be an accomplice. In the last few weeks, he had insisted that once a week she masquerade as him, in blue jeans and his shirt, tucking her hair into the baseball cap and using the wheelchair. Annoyed at first, she acquiesced when she guessed that it was an excuse for him to have a day of uninterrupted repose, when she took his place at the flower shop.

They were both amused at the success of the masquerade. She was amazed at how willing she was to enter into his fantasy life—and, frightened or not, she adjusted. She would live out his remaining days to his scenario. It was all fantasy now. Occasionally, however, the boundaries became blurred and she would then get frightened.

Today was just one more run-through, then—with one exception. Today she would upset the vase of flowers at the precise moment that Hilton was halfway between the candy shop and the bar.

Of course she knew then that this would be a special day, but she did not know for certain, and the authorities could not say she knew, or that she did anything other than what she had been doing for weeks—offering her poor, crippled, dying lover an afternoon of rest.

But she knew! And the evening before, they had argued and fought, wept and commiserated until there was no more energy. And finally she capitulated.

To all intents and purposes his funeral might have been yesterday. Adam had told her that on June 15 he would die, one way or another, and he had asked her as the last gift to co-operate in his choice of death. He would not tell her all the plans, merely that she would have to sit in the booth with her hair tucked up under the blue Yankee baseball cap and sell the flowers for him as she had for weeks before, and which had been carefully documented in advance with friends. That's all she had to know. She was to pretend nothing. To deny nothing. He had meticulously set the stage for her eventual absolution as an accomplice. It was still risky. She was to tell her story as simply as possible.

He had asked her to take his place in the stand and she was used to doing what he asked of her. He had had some errands to do. He had told her to take the wheelchair along since he would follow later on his crutches. Sarah had often done this for him since the wheelchair was bulky and for very short distances he preferred the crutches. Why had she ridden in the wheelchair to the flower stand after being left off by the cab at the entrance to Grand Central? She was to answer she really didn't know. Perhaps a whim. She had wondered what it must be like and curious as to how she would respond to the stares and glances every cripple must endure. She had wanted to get into Adam's skin and see what it must have been for him every day. The baseball cap? It was a common thing for her to wear. It satisfied something in the two of them to dress alike. They had come to look alike, they knew, and it was a kinship. It was, after all, her cap, not his, and she did not know where his cap was. She presumed he was wearing it. He was never without it. And where was he? She didn't know, she was to say. She had left the house before him, as was her wont on Fridays, and had taken her place at the stand.

And indeed she did not know. Adam did not want to describe the final details to her because he knew she would have balked. He had waited twenty minutes after she had left, assuming that whatever surveillance might be on the apartment would now have followed her—particularly since they would have been alerted by Moss of the specific nature of the plan.

Given the specifics, the blueprint, so to speak, of a murder, they were free to concentrate their attention—and concentrate it in the wrong direction! Knowing only that there was to be an assassination attempt, they would have to cast a loose net, but now knowing the who, how, when and what, they could pull their troops in along a narrower line, giving Adam ample room to move along the edges.

He took off his baseball cap, stuffed it in the pocket of his loose-fitting raincoat, and put on a slouchy rain hat. Only one thing more was necessary, and he gripped it in the palm of his hand. The grenade.

It had always been the grenade. With the intuition of a scientist, the right answer had occurred to him first, even before he realized how it could work. Not that the false plot wasn't amusing. But it was too complicated; good solutions were simple ones. How in the world could one be sure there wouldn't be an interceding individual? There was too much distance between him and his victim, and distance invited the unpredictable and the accidental. He smiled, wondering what the police would think when they disassembled the Victorian fern stand and discovered, mounted in among the flowers, a simple child's telescope. Well, he might suffer the reputation of a peeping Tom, and Sarah, since she had no knowledge of it, would be bewildered along with the others. He was amused to think of what her speculations might be as to its purpose. Moss would know, of course, but would Moss tell? He thought not. Perhaps some day Sarah and Moss would sit down and between the two of them, those he had become closest to in recent years, would reconstruct the entire story. He smiled. He liked to think of Sarah and Moss putting the pieces together.

Funny about Moss. At each step he had been an unwilling partner in what was about to happen. The grenade, of course, was at first a stupid idea, as Moss had suggested, indicating all of the ways in which it was a crude and imprecise weapon. But in so doing, he inadvertently pointed out the one way it could be used for certain death. It must be embraced. It could not be thrown away. He attached a leather thong he had prepared around the grenade and hung it like a locket of love around his neck, buttoned up his raincoat and left.

He knew that the difficult part would be walking to the small bar adjacent to the flower stand. In recent days the hundred feet had become, like the last eight miles of a marathon, an almost unbearable distance. He realized that this was his D-day; it had to be today. In another week, he would not be able to make the distance. He had suffered dreadfully getting to the bar and fortunately now had a full twenty minutes to linger over his coffee, until Hilton would make his appearance, and Sarah would drop the large vase of roses.

His heart quickened when he saw Hilton enter the concourse almost precisely on time. He himself had arisen five minutes earlier, not wishing to attract attention at the moment of Hilton's arrival. Hilton began to turn. He stopped for a moment at the candy shop window, wheeled and started to walk directly towards the flower stand. He seemed to be walking particularly fast and for a moment Adam thought he would pass him by before he had made his move. My God, she must remember to drop the vase! Dear God, please let her drop the vase. Drop the vase! Drop the.... The crash came, stopping Hilton in his tracks and alerting everyone else in the concourse, it seemed. Adam could not believe it. With his back towards him, less than ten feet away was Roger Hilton! He had allowed for thirty feet. Only ten feet away! He took one step towards Hilton, pulled the pin on the grenade, lunged forward the last nine steps of his life, almost falling, and embraced the figure of Roger Hilton. Hilton turned with a look of disgust and annoyance, to see the smiling boyish face. He tried to pull loose and the boy clutched to him like a passionate lover as the grenade exploded its hundred fragments into both of their bodies.

Chapter XXV

June 22

The memorial service for Adam Haas had been over now for more than an hour, and Sarah and Peter found themselves still lingering over their second cups of coffee in a small luncheonette just north of the Frank E. Campbell funeral chapel on Madison Avenue. The services had been brief and Sarah had been somewhat offended by the smallness of the crowd until she realized that like everything else, the guests invited, the speakers and the entire program had been prearranged by Adam himself. No member of the family had spoken. Sarah had not been asked. And here, again, she saw Adam's fine perceptive hand. He had known how impossible it would be for her and had spared her the guilt and ambivalence. There were, indeed, only three speakers—and what a strange group they made. Peter Moss, Billyboy Haywood and Professor Solomon Cohen of the Department of Mathematics of Columbia—Adam's original mentor.

And now they sat there, with too much unsaid, yet too little to say; both reluctant to leave. They had talked, each in their own way, of their respective love for Adam, and had remained dry-eyed and surprisingly calm. Now they were talking about the confusing few days before Adam's death, pooling their knowledge and trying to make some sense of his manipulations. Sarah had already been reassured by the authorities (after questioning that was less rigorous than she had expected) that she would not be charged with any complicity in the assassination. Adam had laid his plans well. The fact that she had done nothing more than that which she had done every preceding Friday in the month established a record of spelling her lover that was understandable and sure to gain sympathy. The one unique fact of the day, the dropping of the vase of flowers, was surely an accident that was explicable and could have been uncalculated. Indeed, Adam had planned on this very innocuousness to protect Sarah. Ironically, what he had not planned on, was that in the confusion of the moments before the assassination, no one even recalled that a vase of flowers had dropped. Already, as days went by, the relatively homogeneous early reports were being elaborated into dozens of different scenarios as each eyewitness wove the threads of his own unconscious fantasies into the incomplete threads of memory, creating those personalized interpretations of history that made the past always subjective and essentially unknowable.

Sarah interrupted the silence by saying,

"That foolish Adam, that wise and foolish Adam managed to plan everything and that which he didn't

"Yes, I know," continued Mudd. "But death and assassination seem such crude solutions to problems."

"They are crude, Admiral, and that's why we so seldom resort to them."

Again there was a pause. This time the Admiral broke the silence. "You know I have implicit confidence in you, Hugh. The kind of confidence that makes it unnecessary for me to ask for details in advance and therefore makes it ungracious of me to ask for explanations after the fact. But I was somewhat shocked by the method. Our agents take risks, and risks may mean death, but we have never—correct me if I'm wrong—we have never used kamikazes before."

"You are wrong, Admiral. We did use a kamikaze once. You remember..."

"Oh, yes," Admiral Mudd said, "I had forgotten that case."

"But at any rate, Admiral, I'm sorry I had not mentioned it. The young man was *not* our agent."

"Not our agent?" asked the incredulous Admiral.

"No, sir, it was pure serendipity. He was serving his own private purposes, and his own intentions."

"My God, you mean you left this in the hands of an amateur?"

"Of course not. As it turned out I had no way of stopping his move. He was really quite clever. I had every intention of stopping it. At the same time, it occurred to me that this amateur attempt and the process of stopping it would create an ideal diversion for a more professional attack. The boy was an accident and in this case an incredibly lucky accident. At any rate, with or without him, the mission would have been accomplished. It simply moved our timetable up."

"This means," said Mudd, "that, in this case, with no assassin, the only two people who know about our intentions, then, are you and me."

"The only ones who know for sure. Lowell Stoneham knows, however."

"Why do you say that?"

"He came up to me at the funeral and whispered something to me."

"What did he say?"

"He said, I remember the words exactly, 'You smart son of a bitch, you. Red Herring, indeed!'"

"He's such a smart man. He could have been a good President, perhaps, even, a great one. I'm sorry we couldn't allow that. Too much concentration of power. With all that money—and the presidency—there would be no controls. We just couldn't take the chance. Lowell deserved it, though, and I will always feel guilty depriving him of that which he honestly earned and deserved.

"But," he said, his spirits visibly rising, "that is the past—and Lincoln McAllister is the future."

Chapter XXVII

PERSPECTIVE   by James Saperstein, June 22

> They buried Roger Reynolds Hilton today with the honors and respect due a former President of the United States. And the Hilton haters, the radical roughnecks, the inane ideologues and the decadent dandies of defeat were for once silent. For here, in one heroic moment, Roger Hilton had given his life to prove that which should have needed no proving, that he was a man of courage who placed service to his country above personal needs.
>
> The dramatic and horrifying story of his volunteering in this final mission to make sure that no innocent bystanders would suffer from an assassination attempt on his life was his last service to a country which at this point owed him more than was owed by him.
>
> The historic re-evaluation of Roger

Hilton had fortunately begun before his death, so that those of us who had seen in this complicated man someone more sinned against than sinning could take comfort in the fact that he was aware of the reappraisal of time which would once again elevate him to his rightful place as a major President who served the cause of world peace and through the hysteria of a small fringe had been hounded out of office for crimes that were tolerated in those left of center but were deemed inexcusable from him...

NEW FROM FAWCETT CREST

☐ SHOCKTRAUMA   24387 $2.95
by Jon Franklin & Alan Doelp

☐ DESERT ROSE ... ENGLISH MOON   24388 $2.50
by Claudette Williams

☐ LOOKING FOR WORK   24389 $2.50
by Susan Cheever

☐ THE PASSIONATE ENEMIES   24390 $2.50
by Jean Plaidy

☐ TREGARON'S DAUGHTER   24391 $2.50
by Madeleine Brent

☐ LAST RIGHTS   24392 $2.50
by H. H. Dooley

☐ THE SWORD OF THE PROPHET   24393 $2.50
by Robert Goldston

☐ THE X FACTOR   24395 $2.25
by Andre Norton

Buy them at your local bookstore or use this handy coupon for ordering.

COLUMBIA BOOK SERVICE (a CBS Publications Co.)
32275 Mally Road, P.O. Box FB, Madison Heights, MI 48071

Please send me the books I have checked above. Orders for less than 5 books must include 75¢ for the first book and 25¢ for each additional book to cover postage and handling. Orders for 5 books or more postage is FREE. Send check or money order only.

Cost $_____	Name _____
Sales tax*_____	Address _____
Postage_____	City _____
Total $_____	State _____ Zip _____

* *The government requires us to collect sales tax in all states except AK, DE, MT, NH and OR.*

This offer expires 1 January 82   8152